Hasmonean Preparatory School

בית ספר חשמונאים

THE

LINDA & STEWART SCHWARTZ

KODESH LIBRARY

The Choices of

Daniel Trigo

Joseph Neppe

The Choices of

Daniel Trigo

Joseph Neppe

Targum/Feldheim

First published 1992

Phototypeset at Targum Press

Illustrations: Judy Crown

Published by:
Targum Press Inc.
22700 W. Eleven Mile Rd.
Southfield, Mich. 48034

Distributed by:
Feldheim Publishers
200 Airport Executive Park
Spring Valley, N.Y. 10977

Distributed in Israel by:
Nof Books Ltd.
POB 23646
Jerusalem 91235

Printed in Israel

In memory of my beloved parents,
Nate and Namy,
my father-in-law, Irving,
and my uncle Skei.

Acknowledgements

Thanks to my family: my wife Batya, at my side through thick and thin; Dovid and Esther, Ruthie and Howard, our children, relatives and friends.

And my cousin Dan, whose distance across the sea in America, diminishes not the flurry of our childhood in Johannesburg together, where we ran rampant with games and dreams that imagination is made of — a training that served well in the creation of Daniel Trigo.

In addition to the people of Moshav Matityah, whose support and interest have contributed so much to this endeavor.

PORTUGAL

•Lisbon

•Madrid

Barcelona•

SPAIN

•Seville

ANDALUSIA

•Granada

Allerema

Spain and Portugal
at the time of our story

You Make The Choices!

At the end of each exciting chapter of this book, Daniel Trigo faces several choices. But it's not Daniel who will make the decisions—it's you!

You are Daniel Trigo. You want to save your parents. You want to keep the Torah and mitzvot. You want desperately to do what is right. And it's all up to you.

When you finish a chapter, carefully examine the different choices that are listed. Decide which you think would be the wisest course of action. Then turn to the page indicated to see the result of your decision.

When you've finished "your" story, you can go back to the beginning, make new decisions—and see what happens now!

Good luck on your journey, and good reading!

"Mamma, Mamma, Poppa!"

The family Trigo of Allerema, Spain, had their own special custom on Thursday afternoons. They worked together as a team preparing for the weekly Jewish Sabbath beginning at sunset on Friday evenings.

David, the father, kashered the meat. His wife, Sarah, of noble descent, scrubbed floors and polished the candlesticks. And eleven-year-old Daniel, immediately upon returning home from school, was in charge of preparing the vegetables.

Despite the dangerous waves of anti-Semitism that had plagued the country for many years, the Trigos were a happy family. Tall, refined David was well-known even amongst the gentiles for his kind nature. Beautiful dark-haired Sarah was filled with love for her husband and their only child. Young Daniel, though slightly undersized for his age, had sparkling eyes that seemed to be constantly smiling.

On this particular Thursday in June, 1491, David and

Sarah were sipping tea and waiting for their son, when a knock on the door began the astonishing chain of events that would change their lives forever.

"Strange," David said to his petite wife, with a laugh. "Daniel must be growing up. He doesn't usually knock — especially on Thursdays."

But Sarah sensed that something was amiss. "Wait, David. Don't open!" Her call came too late. He had opened the door.

Before him loomed a small group of burly men, armed with heavy sticks. Daniel recognized three of them to be local peasants. At their head stood a slightly stooped, yet very tall old man. He wore a simple black robe adorned by a large, solitary cross hanging from his neck. The cross glinted in the late-afternoon sun.

"Good afternoon, Don Trigo," said the robed figure, "and your lovely Señorita, too. I hope we are not intruding." His tone made a mockery of the polite words.

Sarah came up to stand beside her husband. They stared at the priest, wide-eyed and speechless.

The Trigo house was situated at the edge of a forest. At precisely that moment Daniel emerged from its thick undergrowth, having taken a shortcut home from school that cut the distance by half.

Catching sight of the carriage outside the house, and the strange-looking men talking to his beloved mother and father, something inside him cried, "Stop!" Gingerly he moved forward and crouched behind a fruit tree, straining to hear.

"Allow me to introduce myself," continued the priest. "I am Fray Antonio Diego, of St. Paul's Church, Seville. By the authority vested in me by our most cherished King Ferdinand and Queen Isabella" — he drew himself up to his full height, fingertips brushing the cross on his chest — "I place you, your wife, and son, under arrest!"

Sarah gasped.

He moved forward and crouched behind a tree, straining to hear.

"With all due respect, Fray Diego," David said, forcibly keeping his voice low and even, "there must be some mistake. We are not criminals. We are law-abiding Jews, loyally serving the Crown."

"Bah! Your efforts of defence are feeble, Don Trigo. Surely, you must know we are not stupid. You have been under suspicion for years, and now finally we have conclusive evidence proof against you."

"We have done nothing wrong," Sarah said defiantly, linking arms with her husband.

Fray Antonio gave her a thin-lipped smile. "Nothing wrong, Donna Trigo?" he sneered. "Let me assure you that you will stand trial, be found guilty, and die at the stake — as will all Jews who cunningly persuade others who have seen the true light of Christianity to return to your evil ways!"

Angrily the old man stepped aside and waved his companions forward to forcibly drag away the arrested couple.

As gruff hands clasped Sarah, her husband's voice thundered forth like a lion's roar.

"Unhand her! We will come with you."

In his hiding-place, Daniel could no longer bear the anguish in silence. He leaped to his feet.

"Mamma, Mamma, Poppa!"

The men turned their heads, and saw a small boy running headlong towards them.

"No, no, my son," David shouted. "Stay away! Run, go!"

Confused, Daniel stopped in his tracks. One leg shot up in the air as he manfully struggled to keep his balance. Spinning around in a full circle, he went crashing to the ground. His mother's screams pierced his ears as he fell.

The jarring thud of impact. Searing pain.

"Oooh, got...to...get...up. Can't move."

A look of horror gleamed in his mother's eyes. It was now or never.

The boy hastily muttered a few words of prayer, tensed his muscles, and with superhuman strength sprang to his feet. Into the forest he fled. Nobody, except for his father, knew the area better than Daniel did. He knew every nook and cranny that might offer a boy concealment. Body bruised, legs scratched and bleeding, he zigzagged through the forest, dodging pine trees, tripping over brambles, gasping for breath — but never stopping in his desperate escape.

Little did Daniel know that his parents' abductors did not even bother to follow him.

"Let him go," Fray Diego ordered his men. "He cannot get far. We'll pick him up later. Right now," he turned back to the Trigo house, "we have more important business to attend to. To prison with these accursed Jews."

The armed peasants surrounded the Trigo couple. Slowly, in solemn procession, David and Sarah were led away.

Deep in the forest, an exhausted Daniel flopped to the ground.

Feeling safe at last — at least for the moment — his mind began to work again. For a time the thoughts whirled aimlessly. He forced himself to relax, to think calmly. His mind finally settled on the concealed cellar where, for years, his parents had taken Marranos to pray and study the holy Torah.

These were Jews who, through bitter persecution, no longer had the strength to practice their religion freely. Outwardly, they became Christians, while secretly remaining true to their own faith. The Trigos, who had managed to withstand the pressures of conversions, devoted much of their time to helping these unfortunate victims. To be caught aiding a Marrano guaranteed death at the hands of the Church.

But despite the great risks, Daniel's parents had imbued him with the preciousness of the mitzvah. His parents had told him never to lose faith. What they were doing was the will of God.

Now, when the dreaded worst had come to pass, he would try with all his might not to disappoint them.

What was he to do now?

Choice 1

Make his way to friends who lived nearby, hoping they were still free. Turn to page 17.

Choice 2

Give himself up, if only for the possible opportunity of being reunited with his parents. Turn to page 24.

Choice 3

Get as far away as possible — to Madrid, where his influential uncle, a Marrano, lived. Turn to page 29.

The Boy-Man

Slowly Daniel picked himself up. He shook his head, dazed. Had he actually fallen asleep? In a flash, the horror he had just witnessed came flooding back. In his mind's eye he saw his parents, surrounded by the priest and his thugs. I can't stay here, he thought frantically. I must do something! But what?

As he brushed the dried pine needles from his pants, his brain began to function again. He had an idea — the most obvious place to go. The home of the Meir family.

The Meirs were his parents' closest friends, and were also involved in many community activities. Fortunately, they lived close to the forest. By venturing deeper into the woody haven, there was less chance of being seen — or so Daniel fervently hoped. He started walking.

Daniel tried not to think of his parents' desperate plight, but the tears trickled down his cheeks. "This is not doing me any good," he told himself sternly. "My main concern should be to get to the Meirs before dark." Resolutely, he quickened his pace. The sinking sun filtered through the leaves overhead, turning the forest floor an orange tint. At the end of an hour's walk, Daniel spotted in the distance the house of his friends.

As he drew closer he noticed that all was still. The house appeared empty, lifeless. He hesitated, uncertain what this meant.

Where were the Meirs? Was the house safe?

Suddenly, a hissing sound reached his ears. It was coming from a clump of bushes to his left. Someone was calling him! Though the voice was only a whisper, it was filled with urgency.

"Daniel, over here. Walk towards me — quick!"

As if in a trance, Daniel obeyed without question. A boy, somewhat older than himself, crawled out from behind the thicket. He was a stranger to Daniel, but his face was oddly familiar.

The boy threw Daniel a searching glance. Then, with a commanding air, he said in an undertone, "I am a friend. The Meirs have been arrested. The lackeys of the Church are waiting for you inside. Come on, we have to move fast." As Daniel was about to speak, the boy gestured for him to be silent. "Follow me; I'll explain later."

Once again, Daniel did not hesitate to obey. Instinctively he followed the lad. Together they sped away from the trap which had been laid to deliver Daniel into the clutches of evil.

Leaving the safety of the forest behind them, the two boys entered the town. They walked swiftly in and out of small, twisting alleyways, keeping away from the main street where early evening shoppers thronged the busy market. At last Daniel's companion stopped outside a house at the end of a side street, not far from the town center.

The building was almost in ruins. Clearly, nobody lived in such a hovel. Dirty, cracked walls and a foul smell greeted them

A boy crawled out from behind the thicket.

as they darted inside. The boy led Daniel to a second room, where he produced a candle from a drawer in a rickety table and lit the wick.

In total contrast to the entrance, the room was spotlessly clean. There was a fire-stove, and some food stacked in a corner. No doubt the place was used as a hideout, Daniel thought in great excitement. His eyes were attracted mostly, however, to two mattresses on the stony, cobbled floor. He was more tired than he'd ever been in his young life. Every bone ached with the desire for sleep.

The bigger boy, watching Daniel, wiped the sweat from his brow and smiled.

"Phew, that was close! Allow me to introduce myself," he said, bowing courteously. "My name is Juan Fedora, from Madrid."

"Of course!" Daniel exclaimed softly. "I knew I had seen you before. We met briefly when I spent a few weeks with my Uncle Sebastian in Madrid, remember? You once lived in Seville. Your family are Marranos." He shook his head in wonder. "It seems so long ago."

"Yes, you remember well, Daniel. It has already been five years since we left Seville to seek a better life in Madrid."

"I don't understand. You were waiting for me? How did you know that I was on my way to the Meirs? Surely, you could not have known so soon of my parents' arrest?"

Juan put his hands firmly on the boy's shoulders. "Whoa, Daniel. Wait a minute. You have many questions, but I am tired. I think we both are. We are safe here. Come, let's get some well-earned sleep before we talk. Who knows when we'll have such an opportunity again?"

At the mere mention of the word "sleep" Daniel felt his legs buckle in exhaustion. There was one question, though, for which he had to have an answer.

"Juan, do...do...you think I'll see my parents again?" A

heavy lump formed in his throat as he spoke.

Juan spoke soberly. "Daniel, you must be strong. Listen to me. We will rescue them together. You must not give up hope." He smiled. "I know what I'm talking about. Two months ago, I had my bar mitzvah. I'm a man now."

Daniel returned the steady gaze of the boy-man standing before him. He felt ready to put his trust into any course of action Juan might devise. He had to trust somebody.

Without speaking, the older boy lit a fire on the stove and heated water. Tenderly, he proceeded to wash Daniel's bruises. Tea was poured, and together they ate some biscuits. Afterwards the two runaways lay down, and within minutes were fast asleep.

Silhouetted in the moonlight at the window, the outline of a bent figure stood dead still. The old woman of peasant stock, wrapped in rags, stood lost in thought. "Those two boys. What are they doing in this old house?" From across the street she had watched them come into view and head straight for the abandoned house.

"Strange...Very, very strange," she wondered. "Jews... is it possible? Perhaps they have done some great wrong to Spain." The old lady's lifelong loathing of Jews boiled to the surface as she edged her way to a window. She tried to peer inside, but her head could not reach the level of the shattered windowpane. Straining her ears, she listened for some sign of life. There was only silence. And then she caught the faint sound of breathing within.

"Aha, they are inside, after all! I will go to the church." She hobbled away, eagerness lending her legs unusual speed.

Before long she returned with two men. One of them — a husky figure of immense size — mumbled jovially, "Of course, there *are* Jews inside. I can smell them." He laughed heartily.

The second man, a priest, was small and wiry. He appeared more thoughtful. "We have to be careful. They could simply be young adventurers, and we'll end up disturbing the sleep of fine, upright Christians. Let us enter quietly."

The locked door posed no problem. It was in such a state of decay, a child could virtually blow it down. Yet the big man regarded the barrier as a fine opportunity to show off his enormous strength. Ignoring his companion's recommendation for a quiet entrance, he stepped back a few paces, lowered his head and charged headlong into the wooden frame. The door snapped open with a sound like the snapping of a twig, and the buffoon was sent sprawling.

In the inner room the two boys woke with a start. Like a jack-in-the box, Daniel sprang up to a sitting position, and froze. Juan, on the other hand, jumped out of bed and grabbed a stick which he'd placed within reach for just this kind of emergency. The intruders burst in.

The big man, who had recovered from his fall, gleefully shouted, "Jews, dirty Jews. I told you so!" Juan did not wait for an invitation. He went into action, swinging his weapon and striking the man a glancing blow in the abdomen which clearly caused pain.

"You little devil," he cried out angrily. "I'll get you for that!" flailing wildly with his hands, he made a grab for the boy's throat, to strangle the life out of him.

But Juan was quicker. He darted past the slow-moving giant and ducked under his outstretched arms. Neither the old woman nor the priest was a match for the youthful speed of Juan Fedora. Vainly, they ended up clutching air.

Escape beckoned — but, instead, Juan turned back. Like a raging bull he hurled himself at the big man. Both of them went crashing to the floor. With all the strength he could muster, Juan pinned down the arms of his dazed foe. The sweat ran down his face from the immense effort he used holding down the giant. Juan knew that the man would break loose in a matter of seconds.

"Escape, Daniel!" he shouted. "Run!"

Daniel came to life. He was out of the room and gone before any of the others could move. When he reached the street he gasped as the cold night air enveloped him. Daniel ran wildly, his thoughts a haze of confusion. The only thing he knew for certain was that, once again, he had to get away.

Eventually he found himself in a deserted dead-end street, with only the back walls of houses to be seen on either side. He stopped to catch his breath. For a while, he would be safe.

For the first time since his mad dash had begun, he allowed himself to think of Juan. In order to allow him to escape, his friend had remained behind with the enemy. Juan must certainly have been overpowered, and was now a prisoner — just like his parents.

What should he do now?

Choice 1

Try and locate his influential Marrano uncle in Madrid, as well as Juan's family. Turn to page 37.

Choice 2

Attempt to round up a group of Jews — no matter how difficult —to storm the prison and free the prisoners. Turn to page 45.

Choice 3

He was just a young boy, after all. Give himself up and hope to be reunited with his loved-ones. Turn to page 52.

The Town Square

The leaves high above swayed in the cool breeze of late afternoon. "I must not pass out," Daniel thought determinedly. He tried to rise, but it was no use. His injured leg hurt too much. The boy finally decided to conserve what little energy he possessed. He lay back.

Even as he rested, his mind buzzed with activity. If he had one wish, he asked himself, what would it be? "To see my parents again," he decided without hesitation. "To be with them."

Perhaps it had been futile to flee. It might have been better to give himself up. He made up his mind then and there. That's it — I'll run no more. Relieved at having made a decision, he fell into a deep, dreamless sleep.

He was awakened a couple of hours later, stiff and cramped, by a cold wind ushered in by the blanket of night that had covered the forest while he'd slept. In the near-total darkness,

Daniel would not have been able to see his hands in front of his face if it were not for patches of moonlight filtering through the trees.

Out of the stillness, came a sound. "Hoot, hoot."

Startled, he turned, but saw nothing. At that moment the whole forest seemed to come alive. Animals, insects, and who-knows-what-else, all began singing together in one gigantic night concert. Alone and frightened as he was, Daniel found a measure of comfort in the sounds of nature.

There was a sudden thrashing in the bushes close by.

"Wolves!" Daniel thought, horrified. People said they roamed the forest at night. A second later he heard a hair-raising howl. Daniel cringed in fear. Was this how it was going to end — devoured by a pack of wolves?

The noise grew louder. An ominous addition joined the chorus: human voices, calling to each other in the darkness! It dawned upon the boy that the howling was not that of wolves, but of dogs. Before he could properly understand what was happening, three men and their leashed canine hunters came into view.

One dark figure rushed at Daniel. A long spear prodded menacingly a hair's-breadth away from Daniel's chest. The young Trigo felt all his will draining from his body.

"Don't taunt the boy," a second man yelled. "We want to claim the reward, not harm him." Daniel looked up at the merciful speaker, and saw a face he recognized. A glimmer of hope flickered in his heart.

"Don Conta, my neighbor!" he shouted. "Felipe, your son, and I go to school together. He is my friend. Please, don't let them hurt me."

The men were struck into a surprised silence. Don Conta spoke up uneasily. "Your family has been arrested. They will probably be burned at the stake."

"And deservedly so," rumbled the man with the spear. He

brandished it as he spoke. "They have been turning good Christians away from the truth. I am not fooled by your sobbing. I wager you are not so innocent yourself!"

"There has been enough talk," interrupted Don Conta. "Let's take the boy to the town square where we are to hand him over to the Church."

Daniel studied him intently. Was this man a savior or an enemy? Could he be trusted? What he saw was a face hardened by years of toil, and devoid of expression. Don Conta betrayed no clue as to his real feelings. Without further delay, the men raised Daniel to his feet. Despite the pain, he yanked himself loose and walked unaided. In short order other groups of pursuers arrived, swelling the ranks of those escorting their prize catch.

By the time the procession reached its destination, word had gotten out that the young Trigo had been caught. Though the hour was late, a large crowd turned out to witness his capture. People milled about. Those that had had dealings with the Trigo family gloated. Others hurled abuse at the young captive. Eventually, a sleek carriage pulled up to the square. An emissary of the Church had finally arrived — and a distinguished representative he was. Cardinal Pedro Bialo, himself.

A large middle-aged man splendidly attired in silken garments, Cardinal Bialo received the roars of the crowd with a raised hand, acknowledging their unswerving allegiance. All moved aside as he stepped forward to cast a steely glance upon the boy. For a moment the boy and the churchman locked eyes.

The Cardinal was the first to turn away. Smiling broadly, he addressed the gathering in a booming voice.

"Thank you, thank you, my dear friends. Your support is most inspiring. I personally guarantee that you will all be suitably rewarded for your outstanding loyalty." Abruptly, he whirled back to face Daniel. "And you, young man — what have you to say for yourself?"

Daniel, thrown off balance by the sudden question, stuttered, " I...I...All I want, is to be with my parents."

"All in good time, my little friend," the Cardinal said blandly. Turning back to the audience, he proceeded to make a speech that took the majority of the listeners by surprise.

"Here, standing before us, is a mere stripling of a lad. The Jew Daniel Trigo is not yet totally responsible for his actions. Granted, there are children his age who are already so riddled with impurities that they are — alas — beyond any hope of redemption. But this boy shows a sparkle. I sense it. Also, I have heard from some folk that he is not fully at ease with the falsehoods of the Jewish belief.

"Therefore" — the Cardinal paused impressively — "I have decided to treat him mercifully. I shall allow him to choose his own destiny." Speaking directly to Daniel now, the Cardinal lowered his voice. "We are a magnanimous people, boy. Kindness and love for all mankind forms the basic credo of our faith. If you choose to accompany me and allow the Church to shower you with Her wisdom, you will find truth and happiness."

Daniel made no answer. The Cardinal smiled benignly. "Perhaps you wish to be left alone for a while. Perfectly natural and understandable. You are surely feeling the stress of your situation." Suddenly, he shook a finger in the boy's face. "But I must warn you! If you persist along the misguided Jewish path, your end will be destruction. And I assure you, Daniel Trigo, that you will never see your parents again — or my name is not Pedro Antigue Bialo, Cardinal of Seville!"

What should Daniel do?

Choice 1

Pretend to be interested and accompany the Cardinal. Turn to page 116.

Choice 2

Play for time; tell the Cardinal he wants to be left alone for awhile. Turn to page 123.

Choice 3

Fulfill the commandment of sanctifying God's name. Inform the priest that he is a Jew for now and all eternity. Turn to page 127.

Carriage of Intrigue

y uncle. My kind Uncle Sebastian, in Madrid. That's
where I'll go."

Daniel vividly remembered a few years back, when he and
his parents had visited the huge, sprawling city in the center
of Spain. How exciting it had been — but also frightening.
Uncle Sebastian was a Marrano, and although a respected
businessman with connections high in the government, he was
constantly being spied upon by the people with whom he came
into contact. As if it knew it had to be at top strength to
undertake the difficult journey, Daniel's young body was heal-
ing quickly from its bruises. Daniel was soon on his feet, making
his way through the forest. His first step would be a risky one.
Daniel had decided to take the chance of entering Allerema to
seek out trusted friends. He must have help in organizing
transport to Madrid. This was not going to be easy.

It occurred to him, as he trudged along, that he had neither money, nor a change of warm clothing for the chill of the evening air, which he was already beginning to feel. But that was the least of his problems. If and when he eventually arrived in Madrid, that's when his real problems would begin. Locating his uncle in a big, dangerous city — especially as a young boy escaping arrest — was not a prospect he was looking forward to. But had he any other choice?

Stepping clear of the forest at last, he came upon a main road. The bright light of the moon and the twinkling of candlelit homes guided him towards the town. He was on his way.

Or so he believed.

Approaching a bend in the road, he heard a rumbling sound. There was a rapid clickety-clack of wheels along the pebbled road, and a carriage swung into view. It was pulled by four big horses, and was moving fast. Without slackening its speed, the carriage bore right down on little Daniel Trigo!

By diving headlong into a thicket of bushes, Daniel narrowly missed being crushed to pieces by the pounding hooves. Startled by his sudden move, one of the horses careened wildly, causing the carriage to tilt dangerously from side to side. The wheels screeched to a halt. The two front horses, alarmed by the confusion, lifted their forelegs high, pawing the air. All four steeds neighed furiously. The driver fought to hold the reins. With expert handling he managed to bring the horses to a standstill. The air was choked with dust as the carriage-door was flung open, and an aristocratic-looking head appeared.

"Driver, what is the meaning of this? How dare you treat our lives so recklessly? I'll have your hide for this!"

The driver answered coolly. "Someone on the road, Count Rodriguez. The horses saw him at the last possible moment." A stirring a few meters away caught the driver's attention. He pointed. "Look, there he is!"

Daniel stood up groggily. His curiosity peaked, the passenger stepped out of the carriage. He was immaculately dressed and boasted a thin moustache. Two other passengers joined him. One was a woman in black clothing, a netted veil covering her face. The other was a young man who, by his shabby appearance, seemed to be a field worker. Slowly, Daniel began to approach them. He was filled with trepidation. The four figures stood still, watching his every movement.

Mustering up his courage, Daniel spoke first. "I'm sorry for what happened. It was dark. I did not see you coming."

The driver wagged a cross finger at him. "Well, you should thank your lucky stars you were not killed. We could have *all* been killed, with you strolling like that in the middle of the road!"

"Stupid little peasant," added the elegant-looking man. "He is lucky I don't beat the living daylights out of him. But there is no time." He snapped his fingers at the driver. "Hurry, man. I must be in Madrid by midday tomorrow." He turned back to the carriage, but his words echoed in the night.

Daniel's pulse raced. "Madrid!" One by one, the passengers returned to their seats in the carriage. The driver resumed his place on top and seized the reins in his hands.

"What are you standing around for, boy?" he shouted down. "Out of the way — or you'll really be trampled this time!"

Daniel gathered his wits. "Uh — excuse me, sir. Do you have room for one more?"

The driver was so taken aback by the unexpected request that he almost fell off his seat. "Another passenger, is that what you mean? As it happens, I do have place for one more. Who is it?"

"Me, sir," Daniel meekly replied. "I am on my way to Madrid."

The driver looked skeptical. "You have money for this trip?"

"No, I don't." In angry response, the driver was about to let down the brake and send his horses on their way, when a loud voice boomed below. The count's head protruded at an angle out of the window. "What's the delay now, driver?"

"It's this young rascal again, Count. He wants a ride to Madrid" — he snorted — "for free!"

"Well, tell him to get out of the way. We have no time for tomfoolery!"

Daniel planted himself before the horses. The animals tossed their heads and pawed the ground, their breath puffing from their nostrils. They were raring to go. He stood firm till the last possible second. The horses plunged forward. Daniel leaped aside. But just as the carriage began to gather momentum, a woman's voice rang out from the carriage. "Driver, stop!"

The driver yanked hard on the reins. With a long drawn-out squeal of wheels, the carriage pulled up short. The carriage door was flung open, and the woman's head appeared. "Tell the boy to get in. I will pay his fare."

Daniel was at the carriage door almost before she'd finished speaking. Amazement and relief joined to make him speechless. Most of all, he was flooded with an immense gratitude to his Creator, for sending this unexpected bit of good fortune his way. His hopes soared. Surely this was a good omen. His quest for Uncle Sebastian would prove successful in the end. It must!

Daniel was seated inside the carriage before the other passengers had recovered from their astonishment.

"Well, I'll be," exclaimed the count.

The farmer was more forthright. "Are you crazy, Madame? He's nothing but a rogue. Why put yourself out for a scamp like that?"

Ignoring the outbursts, the lady sat silent.

Daniel sat next to the farmer. Opposite, the count glared at him. After an awkward silence, Daniel squeaked out a bumbling "Thank you" to his mysterious benefactress. An ever so slight nod of the head, was the full extent of her acknowledgement.

The ice had been broken. The count felt it proper that he should be the next to speak. "I am Count Rodriguez, from His

Majesty's Court in Madrid. I am a cousin of our great Queen Isabella." He peered closely at the boy. "Who exactly are you? And what were you doing in the middle of nowhere, with neither money nor any provisions for traveling? You had better speak the truth." The count, accustomed to giving orders, did not mince words. This young scamp was no match for him. Surely the boy would crumble before his cutting tone, his piercing gaze.

But the count's estimation was wrong. A lifetime of intrigue had trained young Daniel well. Time and again in the past, "chance" meetings had been arranged when he would be approached by individuals from the Church asking questions about his parents. They invariably failed to obtain evidence from the boy. He had trained himself to lie, when necessary, without flinching.

"My parents died in a plague, Your Excellency. I have been wandering alone for two days, with little food and no money. When I heard you were going to Madrid, I reckoned that it was as good a place to find work as any. I have no family left to support me."

"What is your name?"

Daniel began to sob quietly. "I am known as Antonio Sanchez, Your Excellency. My father was a poor shoemaker."

"Is that so?" The count raised an eyebrow, making an already long and aquiline face even longer. "A likely story. I am not a fool. When we get to Madrid, you'll be coming with me, and then we'll find out who you really are."

The thin lips stretched into a smile, but the count's eyes were icy. A cruel man, thought Daniel. Someone who was used to getting his own way, and would stop at nothing to get it...

Believing that he had filled the boy with the fear of death, Count Rodriguez rapidly lost interest. Within minutes he was asleep, as if nothing eventful had transpired during the journey.

"You're in for it now," sneered the farmer. "Would've been better for you to stay back there on the road. Count Rodriguez is well-known for his aversion to criminals, ha, ha."

Daniel shuddered. His good fortune at finding a ride so easily was quickly turning into a nightmare. He cast an imploring glance towards the one person in that confined space from whom he sensed no animosity. The lady, his benefactress, sat very still. Her eyes were closed, and her head bobbed in rhythm with the rocking of the moving carriage. Possibly she was asleep. Or perhaps she was wide awake, knowing full well all that was going on but choosing, for reasons of her own, not to interfere.

The boy was frightened. What to do next?

Choice 1

Get to Madrid and then deal with the count. Turn to page 149.

Choice 2

Escape while he can by somehow stopping the carriage and running — again. Turn to page 155.

Choice 3

Confide in the lady. Turn to page 162.

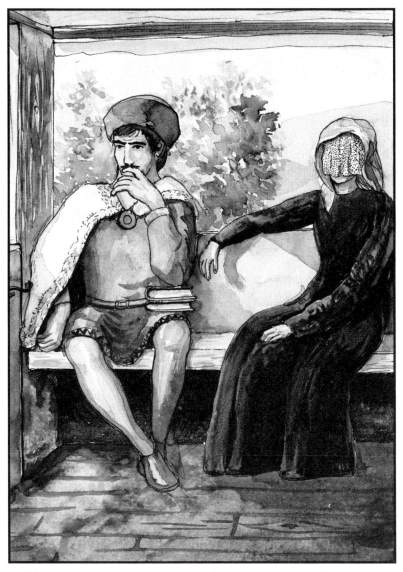

The lady...sat very still...choosing, for reasons of her own,
not to interfere.

Escape to Madrid

The sensible thing to do while he was in the forest was to contact the Meir family. Now, of course, that avenue had been sealed tight. "My only hope is to get away from here. I'm sure everybody is looking for me. Somehow, I've got to get to Madrid — to Uncle Sebastian. He'll know what to do!"

It was not going to be easy. He had no clothes other than those he wore. No money, no food. On top of all that, Daniel was sure that the terminus — where carriages departed for various destinations in the north — would be teeming with people out to get him. "I have to keep to the shadows, and lay low during the day," he schemed. Living with danger caused him to think and plan in a mature fashion that went well beyond his years. Turning, Daniel moved cautiously back in the direction he had come from. How to reach Madrid? He had no answer. But he remembered his beloved father's words: "Nothing ventured, nothing gained." If he stayed rooted to the spot, certain capture would be his lot — or perhaps even worse...

Just moments later, fate took a hand in whisking the boy away from his hometown, right under the noses of almost all the villagers who were searching for him. It happened in this way.

Daniel had walked some 200 meters when he heard voices. He stopped in his tracks. A turn to the left offered the possibility of escape. He took it. The talk receded into the distance.

Silence descended — but only for a moment. Again the sound of human voices broke the night air. Frightened, he spun around. He was caught between stark walls of mortar on both sides. The walls seemed hostile, like the people living behind them in cramped stone houses hidden from his view. He was trapped!

Panic snuffed aside the power of reason. Daniel began to run. Suddenly, two figures appeared in front of him: a man and a boy. Blindly he hurled himself towards them, hoping that the sheer force of his forward momentum would knock them off their feet. He vaguely heard his name, called out in a shrill tone. "Daniel! Daniel!"

Out of the corner of his eye he glimpsed the boy's face. The big, brown eyes and protruding ears brought a wave of instant recognition. He swerved to avoid tumbling into the outstretched arms of those barring his way, and came to a halt.

"Felipe, Felipe!" he cried in near-hysterical relief.

"Daniel, compadre. My father and I, we came looking for you. Everybody is after Daniel Trigo. They think it is funny, but we don't," Felipe said earnestly.

The two boys were lifetime neighbors. They were the same age, in the same class at school. Together, they wept. The tips of their fingers reached out to one another, barely touching — a small gesture saluting a loyal friendship. Felipe's father, Don Conta, stood back.

"To think that I actually considered joining the hunt for the reward," he shuddered to himself. Don Conta tried to shake off feelings of guilt. Aloud he said urgently, "Come children, we must get away quickly!" Without waiting for an answer, he took hold of their hands and began walking rapidly towards his wagon, which stood near the town square.

Villagers approached. A burly stranger demanded of Don Conta whether he had seen the Jewish fugitive.

"No, my two little ones and I are out looking for the devil ourselves," he replied with a haughty air. They walked on. Daniel had to fight the urge to run. Luckily, it was still relatively dark and difficult to fathom who was who.

The square was a scene of bustling activity. Daniel was able to make out the focus of attention. It was a familiar face, belonging to a boy he knew. It was his rescuer, Juan Fedora!

Daniel stopped dead, staring. The crowd hurled abuse at Juan, and threatened to rid the entire land of accursed Jews. Even at a distance, Daniel noticed how tall Juan stood, proud and brave against the onslaught of insults.

Don Conta tugged at Daniel's hand. "Quick, into the wagon. There's no time to waste!" Reluctantly, Daniel obeyed. The three of them got into the wagon, close together, and began the short ride to the Conta residence. As the cart bumped and rattled over the cobblestones, Daniel's heart clenched with fear and rage for his friend. He vowed that some day he would come back to save Juan, the way Juan had helped him, though how or when this would come about he could not even begin to imagine. What could a lonely young Jewish fugitive do against the legions of Jew-haters arrayed against him? Daniel shook his head in black despair.

Later, basking in the warm glow of a cozy fire, his spirits lifted a little. He told his neighbors about his uncle in Madrid, and how much he longed to get there. "I don't know yet how I'll manage the journey," he admitted. "But I believe my uncle is the only one who can help me — and my parents."

Don Conta shifted restlessly on the edge of his soft-cushioned armchair.

"Good!" he boomed. "I'll take you in my wagon. We'll fill it with hay. When we leave the village, you'll be hidden deep inside. No one will find you there!"

Daniel sat up in astonishment. Were his ears playing tricks on him? Why was this man being so kind? The trip would last at least three days, and involve great danger. Though he longed to accept the magnificent offer, he began half-heartedly to protest — more out of politeness than anything else. But even if he had vehemently objected, it would have been to no avail. Don Conta had made up his mind. He was racked with guilt at coming so close to doing an evil deed by entertaining the idea of seeking the reward money for Daniel's capture. To ease his own conscience, he was determined now to help the young boy by any means possible.

"May I come too, Papa?" Felipe pleaded.

"No, no, my boy. Two little ones will attract more attention than is necessary. Besides, you have shown great bravery. I want you to look after the rest of the family in my absence." Although clearly disappointed, Felipe acquiesced respectfully.

After a sound sleep and a hearty meal of bread and vegetables, they set off the next morning. Daniel lay flat and still beneath a mound of prickly straw. He was jarred and shaken by the wagon's uneven progress, but in the stifling darkness he felt safe.

The first challenge came almost before they had begun their journey. At the outskirts of the village they were waved to a halt by three imperious men. Two were dressed in peasant's garb. The third was a priest.

"What have you there, my man?" they inquired gruffly.

"It is only a load of hay, which I'm taking to my brother's farm in Valencia."

The peasants nodded in satisfaction, but the priest eyed

Don Conta suspiciously. "Remove the hay from the wagon," he ordered.

"But Father, with all due respect, it'll cost valuable time to unload and then reload." Don Conta spread his hands in a gesture of innocence. "I am a loyal Catholic. I have nothing to hide."

A gleam came into the priest's eye. A bit of fun would relieve some of the boredom of hanging about a semi-deserted road waiting for something to happen. A pitchfork lay on the bales. "Wait, don't bother doing it yourself. Hand the fork to me instead. I have a better idea."

Don Conta hesitated, and then, reluctantly, did as the priest had ordered.

"Now let's see if you are telling the truth," the priest laughed. He began at first with tentative, jabbing prods that penetrated the coarse yellow straw. Hidden deep within, Daniel flinched with alarm as the deadly pointed edges thrust closer and closer. He squeezed his eyes tightly shut, and prayed.

Then it happened. There was a sudden, searing pain in his leg. A trickle of blood seeped from the soft flesh padding his calf muscle. With all his might, the boy struggled to hold back the piercing cry that was ready to burst from his lips.

Sensing that Daniel was hurt, Don Conta picked up the reins and readied himself to gallop off — realizing full-well that his decision would result in bringing half the province on his tail in hot pursuit. It was at that moment that Divine Providence took a hand.

Totally unaware of the silent internal drama being played out right in front of him, the heavy-breathing priest began to tire from his exertions. "Bah, this is not easy work. A peasant like you probably would not know a Jew if you saw him, anyhow." He gestured roughly in Don Conta's face. "Be on your way, man. If you come across any strange-looking character, pick him up and bring him back to us immediately. Is that understood?"

"Now let's see if you are telling the truth," the priest laughed.

Don Conta's relief knew no bounds. "You need not worry, Father. Can't stand the sight of those heathens myself." Without any further ado, he pulled away from the guardians of the soul, who were as sure as they had ever been that this was one wagon-driver with nothing to hide.

Meanwhile, buried in the straw, Daniel's eyes were blurred with tears. A low moan escaped him, but the jolting motion of the wagon as it began to move, and the heavy load of hay above him, drowned the sound.

Don Conta clucked to his horses. The wagon gathered speed. Though worried about Daniel, the peasant had to be absolutely sure they were well out of sight of the roadblock before he could risk stopping. Only after traveling a fair distance did he permit himself to alight from the wagon. Then he went to work quickly. Frantically he clawed away the hay with his fingers, softly calling the boy's name.

Young Daniel heard the trusted voice of his friend's father. "Here," he tried to shout, but the words emerged as a groan. Don Conta thrust a hand through the last layer of hay and helped the boy up. Anxiously he inspected Daniel's leg.

At last Don Conta heaved a sigh of relief. "It's bloody, but I think the wound looks worse than it really is. The cut is superficial." Don Conta washed the cut with some water out of the flask he kept in the wagon, and dressed the cut with some bandages he took on his travels for emergencies. When he was done, he asked, "How's that, Daniel? How does it feel?"

"Much better," Daniel answered gratefully. Though his leg throbbed, much of the pain was already receding. What had been a stabbing hurt was now only a dull ache.

The rest of the trip passed smoothly. Two days later they arrived in the breathtakingly beautiful city of Madrid. The air was fresh and Daniel scented the heady breath of freedom. Since he did not have his Uncle Sebastian's address, they decided to go first to the home of an old friend of Don Conta's.

"You can trust Carlos Peron only so far," Don Conta warned the fugitive. "For the safety of all of us, I must remind you not to reveal too much. Tell Carlos only what you must — nothing more."

Carlos Peron was a short, stocky man with a bushy moustache and a friendly manner. Safely ensconced in his plush dining room, Daniel asked Peron if he knew the whereabouts of one Don Sebastian Santos.

"Ah, Don Sebastian is a very well-known man in the city," answered his host. He shook his head grimly. "But I would stay away from him right now. He was arrested only yesterday." The words hit Daniel like a thunderbolt. There was a hollow sensation in the pit of his stomach, and his leg began to throb again. He struggled to maintain his composure. "Arrested? Why?"

"There are those who suspect that he is still a Jew at heart," Peron answered in a near-whisper. His manner seemed to say that Don Sebastian had committed a dastardly crime against society. "But why do you want to know, young man? Are *you* perhaps involved with scheming, conniving Jews?" he asked incredulously. The man cast a glance at Don Conta. Its meaning was plain. He did not want anything to do with Jews.

Fighting to stay calm, Daniel rose to his feet. For his own good he could not stay in this house a moment longer. The place was fraught with danger. He thanked the man for his hospitality, but added that he had to leave.

Carlos Peron was only too pleased to be rid of the boy. He left the room, leaving Daniel and Don Conta alone together. Turning to his former neighbor, the young boy said quietly, "You have risked your life for me — more than once. How can I repay you?"

"There is no need. Your family means a great deal to me, Daniel. Your father is a fine man. I am glad I was able to help his son. But what will you do now?"

"I cannot stay here. You know that, don't you?"

Don Conta wavered. He had no plan of action, but knew it would be inadvisable for Daniel to remain in his friend's house any longer. No one in the city knew of the boy's arrival in Madrid. Perhaps it was safe, after all, for him to venture forth alone. He nodded.

"All right. It shall be as you say. Leave at once. But where will you go? Your uncle has been arrested."

"God will help me, Don Conta." Daniel's words were a simple statement of faith.

Don Conta placed a hand on the boy's shoulder as they walked to the front door of Carlos Peron's stately home. "Remember, I'll be here for two more days. If you need me, do not hesitate to return."

Daniel smiled with affection. He put out his hand in farewell. Don Conta's firm grip seemed to infuse him with some much-needed strength. He stepped out the door and into the blinding sunshine.

Where should he go?

Choice 1:

Into the melting-pot of unknown Madrid. God would orchestrate his progress towards safety for both himself and his family — he hoped. Turn to page 60.

Choice 2:

To the parents of Juan Fedora. find them, if they have not also been thrown into prison, and enlist their aid. Turn to page 67.

Aborted Rescue

aniel struggled against a sense of gnawing desolation. "It isn't fair," he wanted to shout towards the heavens. He was only a little boy. He was not supposed to be alone like this, especially so late at night. It just wasn't fair...

Clenching his fists, he fought against the panic that threatened to overwhelm him. This was no way to cope with his plight. "What would my father tell me to do?" he pondered. "That is the question I have to ask myself." Daniel sighed. "If only our rebbe — may his memory be blessed — had not died last year!"

For thirty years Eliahu Kilmo, their rabbi, had carried the burden of woes for his dwindling congregation. Not a day passed when he did not give comfort and restore the spirits of his flock. Little had his people known how the growing persecution was breaking the old man's heart. One day, to the shock and grief of the whole community, this indestructible rock had just died.

"Yes, the rebbe would have given me good advice," Daniel muttered, a tear trickling down the side of his face. "Now I don't have anyone to go to." He succumbed to the luxury of tears — but not for long. With an effort, he shook himself free from self-pity.

"I will just have to free them myself," he resolved. "The rebbe always told us we have to make the effort, and God will provide."

This conclusion came not a moment too soon. At that very second a distant chanting and shouting pierced the air. "Jewboy, Jewboy, where are you? We know you're around here some-where. Come out and give yourself up!"

The sheer suddenness spurred Daniel into instant action. The words "make the effort" pounded at his brain as he made a mighty leap over a wall that, moments before, he would have deemed impossible to scale.

He landed with a thud in a small courtyard at the back of a house. He was trapped — unless he somehow got inside. He had no idea who or what lay inside. Entering those walls could very well mean giving himself up to the enemy. But Daniel felt there was no option. Tentatively, he lifted a hand to knock.

Even before he made a sound, the door opened, as if by itself.

To his astonishment, he recognized the little figure that beckoned him inside. It was Pedro Cadaro, a boy in his class at school. Pedro was a member of a Marrano family who prayed regularly with his father's secret *minyan*.

"Pedro! How could I not have recognized your house! I have been here so many times to play. I am sure our rebbe is interceding with Almighty God on my behalf."

"Daniel Trigo! Of all people!" Pedro stared in amazement. "I heard a noise coming from outside my window, and got up to see what it was." He came closer, a finger to his lips. "Ssh! We must not wake up my family. They are fast asleep. But tell me, how did you get here? We heard that your parents were prisoners and being held not far from here, in De Cilo Prison."

The two boys settled down in the kitchen. In a few short minutes, speaking in a whisper, Daniel rattled off the events leading to his present predicament.

"Well, we must help them," Pedro declared. "We must save your parents!"

Daniel stared at him, bewildered. Pedro began to look irritated at his friend's difficulty in comprehending. He snapped his fingers. "It's simple. We'll round up some of the others and go free your mother and father. What's the problem?"

Daniel found his tongue. "It's not so simple! How can we just free them?" he cried.

"Ssh! You'll wake my parents. We certainly don't want to involve adults in our plan. They'll botch up everything.

"Now, listen. This is how we'll do it. Some of us will distract the guards, while the rest rush past them and find your parents...or something like that."

Impressed as he was with his friend's courage, Daniel was far from convinced that such a plan could work. One thing was sure: he could not stay where he was. In a matter of minutes, if not seconds, the area would be swarming with angry Catholics looking for him.

Without further thought, Daniel gave his consent. "Let's go," he blurted. Pedro did not need any urging. Stopping only to slip on the bare minimum of clothing, he followed Daniel from the house.

Once outside, Pedro took the lead. He knew the terrain like the back of his hand. Darting in and out of alleyways, the boys soon arrived at the home of a third friend. They gave a secret whistle beneath his window, something the boys had once devised — in other, carefree days — as part of an exclusive club. This pattern was repeated at other friends' homes. The whistle did the trick of waking each one up, without disturbing any adults. finally, there were five in all. Each child was a classmate of Daniel's, and a Marrano.

The boys assembled in the moonlight. Pedro, who had assumed command, barked out his orders.

"Right men — off to the prison! The first thing to do is to spy out the land, just like our forefathers did before going into the Holy Land thousands of years ago, remember?"

"Let's hope we are as clever as Joshua and Caleb — not like the other ten spies who were punished for the way they acted," Daniel reminded his fellow warriors.

"Like Joshua and Caleb," shouted Pedro.

"Like Joshua and Caleb," they gleefully echoed.

The other boys were having fun. But for Daniel, this was no game. While the parents of the other boys were fast asleep in their beds, Daniel's were held captive, locked in a dank, dangerous prison.

But for all of them, the stakes were high. Capture meant that all the families would be rounded up. Their Marrano days would be brought to an abrupt and tragic end. Hanging was the usual punishment for the crime of aiding and abetting criminals; "heretic" Marranos were burned at the stake. Not a pleasant prospect, either way...

But Daniel and his friends would persevere. They had to. The words of Rabbi Kilmo inspired him even now, on the brink of his most fateful venture: "Make the effort, make the effort." Moving in pairs to avoid being conspicuous, it was not long before they reached the prison.

The building was the most notable landmark in the town. Until a few short years back, it had served as a splendid castle resort for Isabella and Ferdinand. Whenever members of the royalty spent time at the castle, the town was agog with pomp and ceremony. But the iron fist of the Church and its sweep on offenders — whether they were real criminals, or merely guilty of belonging to other religions such as Judaism and Islam —

quickly brought about a drastic shortage of prisons. With great self-sacrifice the royal family had donated this former bastion of elegance to the Church, for use during their age of tyranny.

The castle's turrets soared skyward. The drawbridge was permanently down over an empty pit, but huge solid doors barred any entry into its inner confines. As the boys stood before the awesome fortress, their earlier mood of light-heartedness evaporated, and gloom settled in its place.

They sat a while without speaking. It was Pedro who broke the silence.

"I...guess I was a little rash in my judgment. It would take an army to break in."

Daniel knew it was time for them to disband, before they really got into trouble.

"My friends, if we are caught — or even seen together — your families will be destroyed. All the years of secrecy, and all the love of Judaism they have instilled in each and every one of you without anybody being the wiser, will be finished, destroyed by the Church. I see now that we cannot allow this to happen."

Heads bowed, they listened. Even now, they would have been willing to do what they could to help Daniel; but he insisted they go home. Their good will and desire to help his parents would forever be a part of him.

He reserved a special farewell for Pedro. "Truly, you have been a Joshua. I pray that one day we all have the freedom to be ourselves."

One by one the boys left, until they were all gone.

Left alone with his thoughts, Daniel noticed that the clouds above formed dark, looming shapes. In happier times he used to watch the clouds form faces, wagons, virtually anything his fertile mind could conjure up. But now, a dark haze spread rapidly across the wide sky. It was like being under a blanket, unable to see beyond a narrow, suffocating world.

Somewhere in that huge, somber block of concrete were his parents. They must be desperately worried about him, their son, and about their own fate. Daniel had never felt so helpless.

His keen ears caught the snapping of a twig, a shuffle. He whirled around, half-expecting the worst. The sight that greeted his eyes was that of a forlorn boy, his own age, but smaller. Someone who had been close to his heart.

"Felipe! Felipe Conta! I don't believe it."

The boy of Catholic descent, who was his best friend in school, found it difficult to speak. "Daniel...I saw you and the other boys pass my bedroom window. I knew you were up to something, so I followed — and overheard what you wished to attempt." Then, after an awkward pause: "Because I am not Jewish or Marrano, I wasn't sure that you wanted me to join you, though I really wanted to help."

Daniel stood up. He went over to his friend, and they hugged.

"You are truly kind and good, Felipe. Thank you."

Felipe had something else to say. He was ashamed. His father, a loyal neighbor of the Trigos for years, had succumbed to the temptation of the reward offered for Daniel's capture. He was probably roaming around right now, searching for the Jewish boy. In a trembling voice, Felipe declared his determination to make up for his father's weakness. "Even if he is prepared to betray you, I never will. I'll do anything I can to help."

Daniel comforted his friend. First of all, he said, Felipe could not be blamed for the actions of his father. "In any case, I am sure that if he really had to choose, he would not betray me. The whole province is caught up in this wave of hysteria against the Jews. Maybe, if I was a Catholic, I would also feel the same way." The relief Felipe felt at his friend's understanding lifted a weight he had been carrying since the Trigo arrest. His voice rose with excitement as he changed the subject to the matter at hand.

"Daniel, you were right not to attempt a storming of the castle. Your parents are well guarded. However, I have some other interesting information.

"Everybody knows that the boy, Juan Fedora, came from Madrid to help you. The whole town is talking about it. I had the good fortune to see a pair of priests take him to a small abbey. They are holding him there." Felipe's black eyes glittered. "Daniel, I am positive that we can get him out!"

Daniel gasped. His heart leapt with anticipation — and doubt. There were so many paths before him, each one fraught with its own dangers. Which should he choose?

Choice 1

Follow his impulse and try and free Juan. If so, turn to page 82.

Choice 2

Decide against it. It would be folly for two young boys to undertake such a hazardous task. Turn to page 91.

Choice 3

Delay making a decision. Perhaps seek further advice or help — but from whom? Turn to page 99.

A Change of Heart

Daniel knew he couldn't stay on that street much longer. His pursuers were closing in. Echoing voices raced towards him through the still night. With only a dead-end in front of him, Daniel was cornered.

The fast-approaching danger numbed his mind. He couldn't think. It was only a matter of time before they would be upon him. Poor Juan had sacrificed his own freedom so that Daniel could get away. If only there were somewhere to go! But even if there were, how could he escape his hunters?

Feeling defeated, he slumped to the ground. *Always think positively*, his father had taught him. He tried now. If he were caught, he supposed, there was a slim chance that he would see his parents again. Mamma and Poppa were good people who meant no harm to anybody. Anybody could see that. His parents were not guilty of any criminal offense; surely they would be released. Catholics, too, were good people. They didn't come any finer than the Conta family, his neighbors ever since he could remember. Surely this horrible episode would have a happy ending. In his wishful thinking, Daniel conveniently blocked out of his reckoning the main cause of his plight: the sinister priest, Fray Diego. The hope of reuniting with his mother and father overrode all else.

"That's it. I'll give myself up," he said resolutely.

His mind made up, Daniel began walking back slowly in the direction he'd come from. Be positive, be positive, he repeated to himself. The words gave him a faint courage. He tried to hold his head high as he trudged right into the arms of the enemy.

Almost immediately, he was accosted by a group of peasants who clearly regarded him as a dangerous rogue. Daniel made no effort to resist when they hauled him to the town's main abbey, where Fray Diego held his ecumenical court. The priest's dark eyes glittered as they looked down on the cowed youngster.

"So, the little boy is caught at last," he said softly to his latest victim. "Would you like to see your parents, Trigo?"

The sight of the priest shook Daniel to the core. The biting snarl in his voice dashed the boy's frail hopes of happiness, but the words offered the reunion Daniel longed for. He stared dumbly at his feet, confused and tongue-tied.

Fray Diego answered for him. "Yes, I'm sure you would like to see them. What a stupid question — how thoughtless of me. Come along, to the castle with you!"

Daniel was paraded through the streets of Allerema, amid the jeers of onlookers who revelled in the downfall of the Trigos. Many other townsfolk, though, remained indoors. Devoted Catholics as they were, they were still stupefied by the cruel treatment accorded their Jewish neighbors. This "silent majority" felt sympathetic, but totally helpless to change matters. They remained behind their shutters, watching. Eventually, as the Inquisition soared to a fever pitch, much of the sympathy evaporated. More and more of the simple folk became willing tools of the Church, infected by its poisonous hatred of the Jews.

But Daniel, passing through the streets with his jailers, didn't think about or understand the gamut of feelings that swept the town. He was hardly aware that his progress served as the day's chief entertainment for his fellow townspeople. Arriving at the castle, he thought of one thing only — his parents. Would the priest keep his word? Would Daniel see them?

See them he did — but not right away. First, he was hauled into an empty cell in a cold, dank dungeon. There was a table and three narrow beds with old and rotting mattresses. A musty odor filled the room. There was no window, just four damp, smooth walls. Daniel looked around him. So this was prison. A place where the outside world did not exist.

He fought a sense of unreality. Who would have believed that he, Daniel Trigo, would end up in this lonely prison cell? Had he made the right decision in giving himself up? How long would they keep him here?

His thoughts were interrupted by the opening of the small, creaking door. His mother and father came into view.

"Mamma! Poppa!" Daniel flung himself into their arms. David and Sarah looked flabbergasted. No one had told them where they were being taken, or that their son was a prisoner. And here was their very own Daniel, in their arms!

At last Daniel stepped back and searched his parents' faces. They appeared haggard and drawn. He was glad to see that his mother retained that aura of refinement that was so much a part of her, despite the harsh treatment to which she'd been subjected. As for his father, though David looked older, that kind and noble face was essentially unchanged. Daniel was reassured. Though beaten and mistreated, his parents' spirits were very much intact.

"Mamma, Poppa. I cannot believe we are together!" Daniel cried unashamedly, and his mother and father wept along with him. They forgot the guards, the priest, the Inquisition. For the moment, all each could see were the beloved faces of the others.

Fray Diego stood in the doorway, peering in. He had been about to cut short the family reunion, but something held him back. The love of the Trigos for one another had a strange effect on the friar. He remained silent, letting them weep together.

In the months that followed, the Trigos were permitted to stay together. The family underwent constant interrogations — sometimes as a unit, or in pairs, or, occasionally, one by one.

Their personal Inquisition took place in a dimly lit room, usually with two or three members of the Church present. David and Sarah were inundated with questions. Time and again, they were urged to confess their "sin" of aiming to wrench Christians away from the true religion. They were also offered the option of "repenting," in order to save their own skins. This, they refused outright even to consider.

When Fray Diego handled the proceedings, he acted out of character. The notorious ruthlessness was replaced by a type of pleading.

"Don Trigo, you must believe me when I tell you that all I wish for is your salvation. Stop being so obstinate. The Christian faith is the true faith. Accept that fact. In doing so, you will earn freedom for yourself and your family."

"Father Diego, I am not the first Jew in this position," David replied soberly. "And sadly, until the coming of the Messiah, I won't be the last."

"But he has already come! He died for mankind's sins. Your wait is futile and worthless."

"Nothing you say or do can induce me to renounce the faith that my forefathers lived and died for, Father Diego."

And so the debate continued.

Seeing that his arguing was not getting him anywhere, the frustrated priest decided he had no choice but to keep the wheels of justice turning. Witnesses, purporting to be acquaintances of David and Sarah, brought trumped-up charges against them. Evidence was mounting.

Rarely, in the ten years of the Inquisition, had one family received so much attention. Fray Diego, without giving any reason, stretched out the interrogations. Some attributed this to a warped delight at prolonging suffering, but David and Sarah were at a loss to understand his peculiar behavior. Surely, in the Church's foul judgment, there was enough against them to warrant the death sentence?

There were times, mostly in the dark of night, when the family enjoyed moments of solace together. David strove to give Daniel strength and hope for the future, though their prospects seemed bleak at best. During those stolen moments, David instructed his son in the ways of the Torah. He found Daniel a keen pupil. Tenderly, he spoke of the Next World, where the children of God basked in His glory. He impressed upon his son that this earthly existence is but a corridor to the eternal home of the Next. Ultimately, whether one lived 120 years or just a handful, this life amounted to a flicker compared to the everlasting eternity of Heaven.

The message David was giving his son was the distinct probability that their earthly life as a family would be cut short. As he spoke, the pain in his voice filtered through to Daniel. Once, David was astounded by his son's reaction.

"Where there's life, there's hope. You know that, Poppa. Our rebbe used to say it all the time." The boy refused to contemplate the possibility of impending death.

They slept only out of sheer exhaustion. There was no time now to give way to the frailties of the human body. Every moment must be spent in learning, in talking, in being together. For who knew how little time was left to them? For the moment, thanks to the delaying tactics of Fray Diego, they were safe.

This situation ended abruptly one day, with the sudden departure of the priest.

"I have business in Granada," Fray Diego informed them. "I am not sure how long I will be away. In the meantime, I have left instructions that you be released at once — after professing your allegiance to the Church."

"You're wasting your time, Father," David said quietly. "We will not budge."

Raising his voice in anger, the friar threatened, "Until now you have been wallowing in luxury here in prison. I cannot guarantee that this state of affairs will carry on much longer!"

Slamming the prison door shut, he stormed out of their lives for two months — months that would prove the most difficult in the lives of the family.

Straightway, the meager ration of bread, water and vegetables, until then brought in twice daily, was cut down to once a day. The underlings left in charge were eager to obtain a confession where the great Fray Diego had failed. Gradually, conditions became increasingly unbearable for the small family, until at last, the dreaded instrument of torture was brought into play.

Sarah was forced to watch as her husband lay suffering on the stretcher-rack. Miraculously, David withstood the bone-crunching ordeal without breaking. Then — to the wailing of Sarah and the vehement protests of David — young Daniel was carried to the rack. It was more than Sarah could possibly bear.

"I confess to criminal dealings with Marranos. In my house, you will find a hidden cellar which we used as a synagogue!" Sarah cried out. David verified his wife's words. He had succumbed. His wife would not die alone.

Before their captors could react, the heavy door of the torture-chamber swung open from the outside. Outlined in the doorway stood Fray Diego. His gaze swept the scene, which told a story that needed no words. He was furious.

"What is the meaning of this? How dare you treat this family so?"

"We don't understand you, Father," his assistants replied in agitation. "You have used far more severe measures on accursed Jews in order to arrive at the truth."

"Yes, well...This family is different. You had no right..." His words trailed off. There was nothing he could say. The confession had been made.

Time passed. Mysteriously, there was still no pronouncement of execution. The torture had longed since ended, and Fray Diego spent much of his time talking to David about Judaism. For example, David would say, "It says in the Old Testament that man is created in God's image. If so, how can you treat non-Christians so badly?"

"Man without the spirit of God within, is no better than an animal," replied the friar. "Christianity is that spirit." He paused, thoughtful. "I do admit, though, sometimes I am so incensed at you Jews that I feel you are beneath the animal. Then, other times, you are nobler than even the greatest of all Christians."

To appease a growing suspicion among his colleagues, Fray Diego mumbled excuses about special plans that were afoot for the Trigos before sentence was passed. His fellow priests were not swayed, nor were they to be distracted. They appealed to higher authorities. And one day, Fray Diego was informed that his own life was at stake if the Trigos were not put to death at once.

On March 28, 1492, Fray Diego decreed that the Trigos were to die three days later.

In somber dignity, David, Sarah and David prepared to leave this world and enter the next. And then — just hours before the execution was to take place — it came. The reprieve.

The King and Queen had signed an edict in Granada, announcing the expulsion of the Jews from Spain.

Confusion reigned in the Church. There were so many prisoners. What was to be done with them? Fray Diego acted swiftly. Before matters could be clarified or an alarm be raised, the Trigos were moved to an area where other Jews awaited expulsion. Daniel and his parents mingled with their fellow Jews, hardly daring to hope that they would indeed be permitted to escape with their lives.

As his eyes searched the teeming mass of people, Daniel came upon a boy he recognized, a boy-man two years older than himself. It was Juan Fedora, in good health despite his own harrowing experiences in prison.

As for Fray Diego, he ended up a hero in the eyes of the Trigos. He was a man, riddled with evil intent, who had changed his inner self after constant exposure to the nobility and truth in a special Jewish family. Knowing for months in advance that the Edict was soon to become a reality, the priest had fought great odds to keep the family alive until that moment.

Fray Diego was not heard of again. Rumor had it that he shed his priestly garb and spent the rest of his life in self-afflicted penitence. His final act had saved the lives of a mother, a father, and a son who never forgot him, or what he had done for them.

The End

Framed!

The cobbled streets of Madrid were far wider than in his hometown. There were so many people hurrying to and fro. For a while Daniel wandered aimlessly. With each passing step he began to feel less threatened than at any time since his parents' capture. He was a stranger in a strange city, where nobody knew him — or cared to, for that matter.

He grew daring. "Mamma and Poppa taught me always to be positive about life. I know what I'll do. With God's help, I'll find Uncle Sebastian and help him get free."

Daniel's thoughts filled him with hope and helped him forget, for the moment, that he was just a little boy. He continued to walk along the streets of Madrid.

He soon chanced upon a large square where quaint modest homes stood alongside elegant spiral towers. In the middle of the square was a busy marketplace, filled with the noise and bustle of people peddling their wares. Trinkets for sale, caged animals to be bought, and all kinds of food, were lavishly displayed. Aromas of spices from different lands and a noisy cacophony of human barterings rose up towards the blue sky. Daniel walked past the different stalls, drinking it all in. No one took the least notice of the boy.

But it was not long before Daniel's anonymity came to an abrupt end.

Three teenage boys came into view, running helter-skelter right at him. Hard on their heels was a group of red-faced pursuers, screaming as they knocked over stalls of vegetables and any other obstacle — human or otherwise — that happened to lie in their path.

"Thieves! Thieves! Stop them!" they yelled.

Daniel tried to step out the path of the boys and their pursuers. He did not move quickly enough. As others scattered in all directions to avoid the oncoming stampede, the young boy was knocked over. He landed in a heap. Just as he fell, someone thrust a heavy, square-shaped box onto his stomach. Instinctively, he clasped it, and then lay still.

In his dazed state he was conscious only of shoes gathering around him. Many pairs, of many different shapes and sizes: some dusty and decrepit, others made from fine leather, and gleaming with polish. All surrounded the crumpled form of the boy who only moments before had been an absolute nobody in their midst.

Afraid to look up at the hostile faces peering down at him, Daniel closed his eyes. He ached to believe he was in the middle of a short-lived nightmare from which he would awaken at any moment.

But reality was not to be denied. At that moment it struck home, with a blow like a sledgehammer.

A hysterical, ginger-haired woman swooped over him, and the object he was holding was forcefully snatched from his hands — so forcefully that the sharp edge of a corner sliced a deep cut

"Thieves! Thieves. Stop them!"

across his chest. The sudden pain seemed insignificant beside the sudden panic that flooded Daniel as the mob seethed and growled with anger.

The frenzied woman tore open the box. Its contents spilled to the ground. Knives and forks, a silver crucifix, and even some odds and ends of food, lay scattered about for all to behold with amazement.

"Aah!" the woman shrieked. "My precious silver cross which I bought for my daughter's wedding! It cost a fortune. Why you little..." Unable to control her temper, she kicked wildly at the boy's head. Fortunately, her aim was erratic, and instead she stubbed her toe on a large, protruding pebble which was part of the square's intricate roadwork. She screamed in pain, and clawed furiously at Daniel. By this time, however, the police had arrived on the scene.

A young man with dark features spoke in a strong voice. "Everybody stand back. Come on now. Boy, can you get up?" Daniel slowly hauled himself to his feet. Realizing he had been caught red-handed as a thief, he immediately denied involvement. "I was just walking through the market, when a bunch of boys came running towards me."

"The lying thief!" shrilled the ginger-haired woman, who had forgotten the pain of her toe. "He is one of the rogues that has been plaguing the market for weeks. Lock him up, Officer — for twenty years at least!"

The merchants, who had suffered greatly at the hands of the elusive gang of thieves, at last had a scapegoat. They craved on-the-spot revenge. The policeman, though, would have nothing of it. "This boy is coming with me to headquarters, where he will receive a fair trial."

The crowd hissed and booed. As they began to voice heated objections, the policeman lashed back at them. "Are we not the most powerful and civilized nation on earth? Why are you behaving like rabble?"

His authoritative air had the desired effect. Before long, Daniel was whisked away to face a fate worse, possibly, than what he would have endured if he had been left to the brand of justice meted out by the ugly crowd.

Police headquarters was housed in a complex made up of three large buildings. The policeman ushered Daniel down a wide, long corridor with slippery red floors. Every few yards there were doors on either side leading to mysterious inner chambers. It was into one of these that Daniel was finally led, trembling. His only consolation was the continued presence of the policeman, who had protected him so manfully in the market. His name was Captain Guy Mendez.

In a room where the only light came from a small window close to the high ceiling, the officer did something quite unexpected. Producing bandages and medicine from a cabinet, he gently cared for Daniel's severe cut. Only when he was satisfied that the wound was dressed properly did he take his place behind the long wooden desk, and begin his interrogation.

"Okay, young man. It's time to talk. What is your name?" An almost overwhelming urge to pour out the whole truth overcame Daniel. He had to battle for self-control. The man was obviously good and kind, but he had a job to do.

"My name is Antonio Sanchez," he lied. "My father, who died a month ago, was a shoemaker. I have never had a mother. My father told me she passed away while giving birth to me."

Guy Mendez's reaction was noncommittal. "Hmm, is that a fact?" He leaned closer the boy. "Tell me, Antonio, did you steal today at the market?"

"No, no! I swear to you, I am innocent. I just happened to be there at the wrong time."

Captain Mendez sat still for a minute or two, not saying a word. Finally, in a quiet tone, he asked: "Where do you live?"

The boy answered promptly. "I ran away from my relatives who treated me poorly, señora." As soon as the words left his lips, Daniel regretted handing the policeman this yarn. The man, he could see, was no fool. Daniel decided to take a great risk.

"Captain, I am not from Madrid. I come from Allerema in the south. I am searching for my uncle." After pausing slightly, he went on. "I was told that he has been arrested."

With renewed alertness, the captain stared hard at his captive. "What is your uncle's name?"

"Sebastian Santos."

Showing no emotion, Captain Mendez informed him that he knew the man. "Interestingly enough, he is in this very building right now. It is within my power to allow you to see him."

Daniel's heart skipped a beat, but before he found a way to respond the captain posed a leading question: "You lied to me. Why?" He was met with stony silence and a bowed head. Undeterred, he went on: "Nevertheless, I perceive that at last you are telling the truth. Antonio, or whatever your name really is, I believe it will be in your own best interests to fully unload the burden you are carrying. Perhaps I can be of greater assistance than you realize."

Daniel hesitated a moment. Standing before him was a law-enforcement officer representing a King and Queen who were instrumental in the widespread persecution of the Jews. How could he trust such an official, even though he appeared honorable and just?

As if reading the boy's mind, the captain continued, "We are living in dangerous times, boy. If you have something to hide, better it does not fall into the wrong hands. Information pried from your lips — and there are ways to make people talk, believe me — could spell disaster for you." Bending towards the boy, he implored him to place his trust in somebody. It was then that Daniel realized for the first time that Captain Mendez was a handsome man. He even bore a marked resemblance to his very own father!

The spark of affection induced by this minor revelation prompted his decision. He was going to confide in the policeman. Clearly, there was no other choice. With God's help, all would be well.

Turn to page 74.

The Mitzbah of Kindness

It suddenly dawned on Daniel that there was another lead he could follow in his quest for help. The Fedora family.

He barely remembered Juan's parents, but if they were anything like Juan, they'd begin to think of a plan immediately to save his parents, as well as their captured son.

Daniel turned quickly to see the door closing as Don Conta went back inside. He would need help to find the Fedoras, as he didn't know where they lived; and Madrid, unlike his home village of Allerrema, was so big. So, gathering his courage, Daniel knocked on the door and was led back to the room where the two old friends were sharing a drink. Don Conta looked up in surprise, while Peron said irritably, "Well, boy, what is it now?"

"Excuse me for interrupting you again, señora," said Daniel politely. "I just needed to ask Don Conta something before I left." Turning to his friend's father, Daniel asked, "May I speak with you in private? It'll only take a minute."

"Why, yes, of course," replied Don Conta. Turning to his host, he added, "You have no objections, do you?"

Carlos Peron, owner of the house, fidgeted in his seat. He was clearly made uncomfortable by the intrusion. Don Conta realized that he was having difficulty with divided loyalties: to an old friend, and to the Crown. Don Conta could understand Peron's dilemma. Whenever strife and calamity struck the sunny shores of Spain, Jews were the ones who were blamed. Why, Don Conta himself had been tempted at an earlier stage to seek the reward for Daniel's capture.

Deciding it was more prudent not to wait for permission, Don Conta took Daniel aside. "Speak, child. The sooner you leave, the quicker my friend will be restored to his old, jolly self."

Daniel ventured the idea of contacting the Fedoras. Perhaps Don Peron knew the whereabouts of the family? Should they risk asking him?

Don Conta knew them from the old days in Allerema. "A fine, upstanding family," he nodded. "I think it's a good idea. But as for inquiring of my friend, definitely not. A change has come over him since I was last here. If he knows who they are, he may be tempted to inform the Church of your interest. Since they are Marranos, this would be dangerous for them. It is better to take a chance looking for them on the outside," said Daniel.

"Then, dear Sir, I will be on my way, and trust in God that I am successful."

"You are a brave lad, Daniel. Remember what I said. I'll wait here for the next two days in case you need me. God speed."

Peron came up on them quietly. Had he overheard any of the conversation? Daniel wondered. He felt relieved as the door closed behind him again and the wholesome, morning air brushed his cheeks. For a few moments, Daniel stood still, not knowing which direction to take. "I'll go where God sends me," he decided. Still, his legs awaited instructions from his brain. All at once, the door behind him opened, and the large figure of Don Conta appeared.

"Heaven be praised that you have not yet wandered off," he said quietly. "At the last minute I could not bear the thought of your going off alone, so I took the chance of asking Carlos if he knew of the Fedoras. And, guess what, dear Daniel? He knows them well!"

Daniel could hardly believe it. "But isn't there a chance he may go to the police with the information?"

The big man dropped his voice to a whisper. "I am only afraid of God, not of man's treachery. In any event, if he proves not to be such a good friend, I have my methods," he said, showing a well-rounded fist to his young charge. "But never mind him, Daniel. I still haven't told you the good news. They live on this very street, just four houses away on the opposite side."

"You mean to say that in this huge city, Juan Fedora's parents are so close?" Daniel asked incredulously.

Don Conta smiled broadly. "That's right. Isn't it absolutely amazing? What a coincidence!"

Daniel was eager to dash across the street, but he felt compelled to pass something important on to his old neighbor. "Don Conta, my father taught me that there is no such thing as coincidence. Everything that happens, comes from God."

The man nodded sagely. "You speak wisely for an eleven-year-old. Now be off with you — before you have me converting to your religion."

Daniel whooped with delight. Chuckling, Don Conta retreated quickly inside before Peron saw him talking to the boy. Little did he realize that his so-called friend had been watching the two of them from behind the curtain of an upstairs window...

Daniel, meanwhile, found the house easily enough. His

optimism deserted him temporarily as he knocked on the door. Was this the best route to follow? Would the Fedoras be the instruments to help him rescue his mother and father?

Before he could do more than entertain his doubts, the door was cautiously opened a crack. Daniel caught a glimpse of a white-haired woman, her face lined with wrinkles. He was taken aback. Years before he had seen Donna Fedora, but in her present state he would not have recognized her. She had aged well beyond her years.

Daniel had changed, too. He was taller and much older-looking than when she'd last seen him. Speaking quickly, he introduced himself to the astonished old woman. She gaped at him for a second, before hastily pulling open the door and letting him in.

A tall man, Juan's father, joined them. Daniel poured out the story of their son's deeds. Juan was the youngest of the Fedora children. The others, all grown-up, had gone their separate ways. It was plain to see that the recent bar-mitzvah boy was the apple of his parents' eyes.

When Daniel was finished, they both began to weep softly. Daniel was told that Juan had disappeared from home a week before. His parents had no idea how and why he was in Allerema. Their lives had been thrown into turmoil as they'd feared the worst...At least now they knew there was a chance he was still very much alive. "We must save him — but how?" They gazed imploringly at Daniel.

"Your son is a man now," Daniel told them. "Don't worry, he will stand up to all the evil until we can somehow rescue him." As Juan's mother burst into a fresh storm of tears, he added staunchly. "God will help us."

Turning away to give Donna Fedora some measure of privacy in her grief, Daniel took in the trappings of the house. Religious articles were prominently displayed. A cross hung on the wall; a copy of the so-called New-Testament lay alongside the Bible. Juan's father observed the boy's repugnance at seeing these symbols of a religion that had dedicated itself to destroy his own. "Daniel, do not be alarmed. We are true Jews inside. We believe with all our hearts in the Torah of our forefathers. But, like so many others, we have succumbed to the forces that threaten our lives. If we had not openly become one of them, we almost certainly would not have survived."

Daniel nodded, but made no answer. In these difficult times, each Jew made his own decisions, and tried to live by them as best he could.

During the next two days, the Fedoras thrived on the comfort and strength Daniel provided them. Vital as his mission was, the mitzvah of kindness to his fellow Jews in times of distress had to be fulfilled. He tried to make up to them for their beloved absent son, Juan. During this time, too, they racked their brains to come up with an approach that could lead to the release of their loved ones. Though they failed to find one so far, the days passed peacefully.

This interlude was brought to an abrupt end by a sharp knock on the door during lunch. Instinctively, the wary conspirators knew that the single thump spelled trouble.

Daniel was quickly taken to the Fedoras' small bedroom, where he hid under the bed. Trying to appear relatively calm, Don Fedora opened the door.

It was just as he had suspected. Two priests stepped into the house. They told the Fedoras that they were engaged in a routine check to ensure that there was nothing un-Christian about their home. Even though the family had long since converted, the authorities still paid unexpected calls on Marranos — occasionally catching unfortunate souls red-handed at their secret Jewish practices.

Though the priests, finding nothing out of the ordinary, soon departed the house, Daniel took their visit as his cue. It was time for him to move on.

As his two days with them had shown him, the Fedoras could not assist him in any rescue operation. It was up to him. Don Conta was still down the street. He would return there first, and see if the situation had in any way changed. Then he would try to figure out his next step.

The Fedoras were sad when Daniel informed them of his intentions, but they saw the wisdom in his decision. They'd been strengthened and invigorated by his visit. Reassuring the couple that their Juan would one day be restored to the family, Daniel took his leave.

He made his way to the home of Don Conta's friend. The door was ajar. He entered a deserted house. Where was Carlos Peron? And even more important to Daniel — where was Don Conta?

Unbeknownst to him, Don Conta had taken matters into his own hands. Having little trust left in Carlos Peron, he had hit upon the best way to make sure Peron did not cause any harm by informing on Daniel. The gentile neighbor of the Trigos had braced himself, breathed deeply, and had suggested a visit to the local bar.

At first Peron had protested, saying that this was not the way gentlemen ought to pass their time. But Don Conta had special gifts when it came to the art of persuasion. After three days of merry-making, Don Conta had returned to see if there had been any word from Daniel. There was no message, and the boy was nowhere in sight.

Don Conta then ventured to the Fedora home, where he was told that Daniel had left a day earlier. Don Conta was baffled as to the boy's whereabouts, and more than a little worried. But he realized that there was nothing else for him to accomplish in the big city. He went home with a headache, happy that at least Daniel had not been betrayed. Befuddled by drink, Peron had all but forgotten the boy's existence.

Failing to find Don Conta, Daniel felt there was only one place to go: to find his uncle, somewhere out there in the vastness that was Madrid.

Turn to page 60.

Reunion

"I am a Jew — from Allerema," Daniel began. "My parents were arrested by the Roman Catholic Church. My name is Daniel Trigo."

Captain Mendez rose from his chair, eyes gleaming. "Just as I thought. Come with me."

The corridors were alive with people. Policemen, clergymen, noblemen and ragamuffins seemed to pop out of walls. Purposefully, the captain walked his charge through the hustle and bustle. Suddenly he stopped in his tracks. A dishevelled, tired-looking man who succeeded nevertheless to carry himself in a dignified manner, was making his slow way toward them.

"Don Santos," the Captain exclaimed.

"Aah, Captain Mendez. It is good to see you. Thank God, I have been cleared of any wrongdoing. It has been finally decided that I am as loyal a Christian as the next man."

"Congratulations!" the police officer said, with genuine pleasure. Then he pointed to the boy beside him. "Don Santos, do you know this fellow?"

Daniel had recognized his uncle immediately. With an effort, he held back his tears as the man, who had hardly noticed the boy's presence, glanced at him with a weary knotting of his forehead. He let out a gasp of disbelief.

"Daniel! Daniel Trigo, the son of my brother! Heaven, be praised!" Unable to control his pent-up emotions for a second longer, the little Trigo rushed up to his relative, nearly bowling him over with the impact of his embrace. The tears began to flow — on both sides. Absorbed in their reunion, they threw caution to the winds.

But only for a moment. Sebastian Santos was a Marrano. People were milling about. If it were known in Madrid that this distinguished figure had — immediately after being released from custody — hugged a Jew, his future would hang precariously in the balance. Captain Mendez was aware of this, but it did not, apparently, concern Daniel's uncle too much. It was only after a few joyous moments had crept past that Sebastian gently released the boy. This gave Captain Mendez his cue to make an official statement.

"Don Santos, I am placing the custody of this child in your hands. God speed you both." The policeman winked, smiled, and disappeared down the corridor before either of them could offer any kind of thanks.

Sebastian Santos gazed after him. "There goes a *tzaddik*, Daniel."

"What? Do you mean to say that...?"

"Yes, my young man," Uncle Sebastian whispered. "He is a Marrano, like myself. And a Jew at heart, like myself, too." As Daniel made to speak again, he put a warning finger to his lips. "Sssh — here we don't say such things. It is our secret."

Uncle and nephew started down the corridor. "Come, Daniel,"

Sebastian urged. "Let us not waste time. In my house we'll be able to talk without fear."

News travelled fast, even in the fifteenth century. Even before Daniel's arrival in Madrid, Sebastian had received word of the fate which had befallen David and Sarah Trigo. Any plan he might have devised to secure their freedom had been thwarted by his own arrest.

After an emotional greeting with Daniel's aunt, Donna Maria and his five Santos cousins, Sebastian and Daniel retired to the drawing room of the luxurious villa, where Daniel excitedly related everything that had happened to him, starting with the horrifying scene of his parents' arrest. He heaped lavish praise on his friend Juan Fedora, and the Conta family.

When his tale was done, Sebastian sat for several moments in a thoughtful silence.

"I, too, have had a narrow escape, Daniel," his uncle said. "It was owing to the intervention of King Ferdinand himself that I was set free — at least for the present. I have many enemies in Spain, my boy. Jews across the length and breadth of the country are in danger. Rumors are afoot that in the near future all Jews are to be expelled from our beloved shores — hard as that may be to grasp. It is only because of my skills at international commerce that the queen tolerates my presence." He frowned. "I am almost positive that she harbors suspicions that I remain a practicing Jew. There is no love lost between Isabella and me. Come the first opportunity, she would have me killed."

A spasm of foreboding gripped Daniel as he listened. His uncle was still powerful — but for how long? Could he help his parents?

As if reading the boy's thoughts, Sebastian told him there remained hope for the Trigos. It would not be easy, he added, because David and Sarah had lived Jewish lives and would never compromise their faith. For them to become Marranos at this late stage would be doubly dangerous. "I will go the king and ask him to authorize their release. I cannot guarantee results, of course, but I will try with all the means at my disposal. We must pray hard, Daniel. In the meantime, you must stay here. It would be dangerous otherwise."

Sensing the boy's disappointment, Sebastian gave him an encouraging smile. "It is important that those who are not in the thick of things give spiritual support to the ones at the front. Besides, I have a further surprise for you," he went on. "While I am away, you will be able to daven with a minyan in my secret shul."

Daniel knew there was no point in arguing. He had to be patient. But he did have one more request. Could his uncle also try to do something for Juan?

His uncle nodded. "That was my intention all along. Another surprise. I forgot to tell you that his parents are part of our clandestine minyan." With those words, he took his leave.

Daniel returned to the main part of the house to play with his cousins.

Several days later, the family received wonderful news. The king had agreed to sanction the Trigos' release! Flattery and bribery, a scheming mind, and a firm conviction in the purity of his mission were Sebastian's tools. He had used them impeccably.

With a small entourage he set off for Allerema, expecting to return within a week with his family under his wing. During the journey, Sebastian recalled one of the things Daniel had told him before he had begun his quest.

"There is a priest who arrested my parents. I only heard his name once, but it is one I cannot forget. He calls himself Fray Antonio Diego. He is powerful and very, very dangerous." Sebastian would have to be wary.

Almost two weeks had elapsed since Daniel's uncle had set out for Allermo. So far, he'd sent no word. Daniel was anxious.

"Don't worry," his Aunt Maria soothed. "They'll be back soon. Call it woman's intuition, or whatever. I feel it in my bones. Come, let us say another Psalm for their safe delivery."

These words gave Daniel the strength he needed. Late that night, lying in bed in a room he shared with two of his cousins and unable to sleep, Daniel heard a faint rumble in the distance. He took it to be thunder.

The sound grew in intensity. Seconds later, it became the distinct cloppety-clop of galloping steeds. Agile as a cat, Daniel jumped out of bed and ran as fast as his legs could carry him down the stairs. Donna Maria had somehow beaten him to it, and was in the process of unlocking the barred doors.

"They're back!" she cried. "They're back. I'm sure of it!"

"Could it really be? Oh, please God." Daniel squeezed his eyes shut, murmuring a quick prayer.

A carriage drew up before the house. One of the doors opened. Out stepped Sebastian, followed by three other people. Daniel, his legs wobbly with excitement, peered through the open doorway. There were the familiar and unmistakable outlines of his father and mother, and the lithe frame of a young boy. It was Juan Fedora.

Bursting with happiness, Daniel rushed forward. After the trials and terrors of the last days, he was filled with the sweetness of life. His one burning dream had come true: to be reunited with his parents and the boy who had rescued him.

There had been times during his ordeal when he'd had to draw on deep reserves of faith to keep going. God was now bestowing the reward.

The Trigos and the Santoses talked into the small hours of the morning. David, a jubilant but gaunt version of his former self, told how he and Sarah had been separated part of the time. Heading the interrogation was Fray Diego, who went back and forth between the two stating how the other had finally admitted to robbing people of their souls. Neither had at any moment

His one burning dream had come true: to be reunited with his parents.

believed the priest, who eventually resorted to more forthright means of extracting their confessions. Torture...

David had been first. But no matter what they did to him, he would not give up — praying to God all the while, before passing out. Then the priest decided to use his trump card: torturing Sarah, in front of her husband.

Such had been Daniel's initial joy at seeing his parents that he had failed to notice how frail they both had looked. David, especially, had aged considerably. His hair had gone mostly grey and his face was gaunt with suffering. David felt his son's anxious gaze. He broke out in a wide grin that made him look almost like his former dashing self. "Don't worry, my son. It won't be long before I will be as strong as ever." He then proceeded with his tale. "It was only our concern for you that had kept us going all along. The sight of Sarah being subjected to torture would have been more than I could bear. I was on the verge of confessing whatever they wanted." He shook his head in bemusement. "Inexplicably, they gave us two days alone before starting the torture. Probably a psychological move.

"On the day the torture was to commence, the dawn rose grey and dismal. We were ready to sign on the dotted line, to admit whatever they wanted. Then, a miracle happened! Out of the blue, my brother arrived, in all his glory."

Sebastian took up the story. "Despite my letter from the king, I had been hampered in my efforts to see David and Sarah. It was four days before I got through to them. In the end there was no answer to the power of the king's order. Once I got inside, the Church had little option but to release the family. Fray Diego mouthed curses, and swore he would not rest until we all paid with our lives."

His wife muffled a tiny shriek. He smiled at her. "Do not be alarmed, my dear. I was ready for him then, and I will be ready for him if he tries something again. God was clearly on our side through all."

"And Juan?" pressed Daniel. "How did you get him out?"

His uncle shrugged. "Once I'd obtained your parents' release, Juan's was no more than a formality."

Juan, who had been sitting beside Daniel quietly listening to the adults, smiled happily. The two boys clasped hands. For a fleeting second, Daniel wondered — not for the first time — how his brave friend had known to wait for him outside the home of the Meir family those few short weeks before.

"I'll tell you one day," came the reply, when he put the question a little while later. Daniel suspected that Juan's reluctance to tell him was due to his innate modesty. He did not want to focus undue attention upon himself.

The family's happiness increased when Juan's parents arrived. They came in full of hugs and kisses for their son. A terrible epoch in all their lives had come to a close.

But persecution raged on in the fearful age of the Inquisition. The Santos and Fedora families remained, in the eyes of the outside world, dedicated Christians. The Trigos continued to live openly and proudly as Jews in Madrid. In a few short months, however, their lives, and that of every Jew in Spain, was changed forever.

On July 14, 1492, the Edict expelling Jews from Spain was decreed. The Trigo clan was once again shaken to its core. And yet, upon receiving the news, there was no braver family in all of Spain than Daniel Trigo and his parents.

What was most important for the boy, who had just celebrated his twelfth birthday, was that the family was together. They were a part of the Jewish people, and would together endure the test that God had placed before them. The Trigos were ready to stand by their brothers and face the difficult future with faith and resolve.

The End

Fire!

"Make the effort, make the effort." Again, the words of his rebbe echoed in Daniel's head. "It's worth a try. Let's do it!" he declared.

For the best part of the day, the two boys nestled under a gigantic tree in a forest. The warm sun, filtering through puffy white clouds, soothed and rested the exhausted Daniel. Felipe Conta had brought along food. They ate, slept in snatches, and planned a strategy. One idea after another was rejected as unworkable. At last, huddled together in the gathering darkness, they settled on their plan. They would break into the abbey this very night!

The boys from Allerema made the hazardous trip across town to the abbey. By now, Daniel had become used to avoiding people, and he passed on this knack to his friend. After a few uncertain moments — once they had to leap trembling for cover behind a wall — they eventually arrived at their destination, unseen.

Fortunately, the building stood close to a clump of trees in an isolated spot on the outskirts of the town. Hugging their cover, they crept on all fours to scout their surroundings. Candlelight shone dimly from an upper window of the two-storey complex. Like centurions standing guard, a series of tall pine trees lined the front entrance. A thick foliage of leaves blotted the light from a full moon bobbing in and out of dark clouds. The darkness was nearly complete.

Daniel peered up at the forbidding building. There was no certainty that Juan was still inside. He could already have been hauled away to a far-off dungeon from which escape would be virtually impossible.

Nevertheless, they must "make the effort."

Both boys called on their reservoirs of strength. Daniel put his trust in God, and remembered the advice of his old rebbe; Felipe gained confidence through the deep and loyal bond he felt with his lifelong friend.

It was time for action. They stealthily skirted the building's perimeter, which was much smaller than the mammoth castle which had confronted the would-be rescuers less than twenty hours before. In the darkness, Daniel tripped on some largish stones. He picked up a few and put them in his pocket. Juggling their smooth surfaces in his fingers, he mused, "Who knows? They just may come in handy."

Gaining entry was not going to be easy. Twice they circled the building, to no avail. Felipe was about ready to give up, when he saw that one window was slightly ajar — on the ground floor too! "What luck," he whispered, eyes gleaming in the dark.

"Let's see if we can pry it open."

The boys crept silently — or so they thought — towards the window. They were still several meters away, when a screeching noise directly above their heads froze them in their tracks.

Had they looked upwards, they would have seen a man's

bald head sticking out of the lit window. Scowling, he drawled, "No, I don't see anything. It's much too dark. Must be those cats again. I wish we could drown them all!"

From inside, a second voice, much calmer, was heard. "Now, now, Father Ambrosio, control yourself. All of God's creations serve a purpose."

"Bah! I suppose so, Father Diego. It must be that I'm a little jumpy. That Jewboy we have here makes me uncomfortable."

The conversation ended abruptly as he slammed the window shut with a bang.

Daniel lay filled with fear. The mere mention of the name *Diego* sent a shiver up his spine. But he was excited at the same time. The man had said, "that Jewboy we have here." True, Juan was a Marrano — but who else could he have been referring to?

Juan must still be here, held prisoner inside that grim fortress. What a stroke of good fortune! The image of Rabbi Kilmo appeared, smiling, urging him onward. His fear decreased, replaced by a steadfast belief that right would ultimately triumph over evil. With a warning finger to his lips, Daniel prodded a frightened Felipe to keep going.

Slowly, with infinite caution, they inched forward again. They were under the window in seconds. Daniel reached up and slipped open the carelessly fastened latch. They clambered inside. Now, to locate Juan.

The boys found themselves in a large, dim hall. They groped through the dark, breathing in the dank atmosphere. But it was the creaky floorboards that worried Daniel most. Each step sent warning signals throughout the abbey. He stopped walking — too late.

A blazing flame lit up the hall, as a familiar figure carrying a torch confronted the bewildered pair. "So, what do we have here? Aah, young Trigo, I see — and a little companion. Well, well, how touching...and what a pleasant surprise."

Daniel...slipped open the carelessly fastened latch....
Now, to locate Juan.

Daniel stood dismayed before his family's most bitter enemy. Rage rose up in his throat. He wouldn't let Father Diego win again — he wouldn't! With sudden inspiration, he thrust his hands in his pockets and pulled out one of the stones he'd put there. Drawing on all his strength, he hurled the stone right into the mocking face of Father Diego.

His move caught the priest by surprise. Like the pebbles that David catapulted against the giant Goliath, the stone landed dead on target, striking Father Diego a fierce blow on the cheek.

The priest yelped and brought a hand to his face. The sting caused him to release the torch, which dropped onto his sandalled feet. A spark ignited the long dark cassock he wore.

With a scream of agony, Father Diego scampered towards the washroom, and water. In his haste he brushed against a flowing curtain, which seemed to suck the flames into its silky depths. Within seconds, a fire was raging in the hall.

As Daniel and Felipe stood transfixed, a second priest ran into the hall. He stopped short, staring at the leaping flames. The priest covered his face. "My abbey, my beautiful abbey," he moaned.

Daniel quickly gathered his wits. "We'll help put out the fire!" he shouted. "But we need more help. Quick — get Fedora!"

"What's that?" Father Ambrosio stammered, gaping at the boys. "What's that you say?"

"Juan Fedora, your prisoner. He can help put out the fire. We need every pair of hands we can get."

As if in a trance, the priest pointed limply to an upstairs room. Daniel started towards the stairs. "Wait, wait," called the priest. "Here's the key. And hurry back, oh, please, hurry back. We've got to save the abbey!"

Daniel grabbed the key and charged up the stairs, with Felipe close behind. The fumes had preceded them. The boys gasped for breath as they ran. They reached the upper corridor. A furious knocking was coming from one of the rooms. Daniel caught a faint cry from within.

"I'm coming, Juan, I'm coming! Hold on!"

Daniel's hands shook as he tried to turn the key in the lock. All at once, the door swung open. His friend, Juan, the boy-man, emerged.

"Daniel!" With a huge, toothy grin, Juan Fedora opened his arms wide. They hugged, and separated almost immediately. Time was running out.

"Hurry, we must get out of here!" yelled Felipe.

Covering their mouths with their hands to stop the billowing smoke from penetrating their lungs, the boys raced down the stairs. In the hall they encountered a hysterical Fray Diego, hurling abuse at his fellow churchman. "Fool, you absolute fool! Why did you give him the key?"

The abbey was burning all around him, but Fray Diego was undeterred. Jews were on the loose. Nothing else mattered.

"Come on!" shouted Juan. His friends did not require a second invitation. In a burst of sustained energy they bolted passed the priests, through the inferno that had once been an abbey. Fray Diego made a belated, stumbling effort to pursue them — but to no avail. They had raced beyond his reach.

The night air was blessedly cool after the heat and smoke inside the abbey walls. The boys ran until they had put the place well behind them. Then, in the shadow of a copse of trees, they stopped to catch their breaths, and decide on their next move.

All three needed attention for minor burns. They decided to make for Felipe's house, despite the danger of Don Conta's presence. Their progress was slower now. They were tired. By the time they arrived the sky was lightening at the edges. It was almost dawn. They entered slowly, not wanting to wake the sleeping family.

To their utter astonishment, two men were sitting at the table in the dining-room.

One was Don Conta, who held his head in his hands in a melancholy way. He looked up at the unexpected arrivals, and gaped. The other man, a stranger, had been talking animatedly, hands waving in all directions. He ogled the boys as if they were an apparition from the heavens, his arms still suspended in mid-air. He was literally speechless.

Juan was the first to regain composure. "Don Sebastian, is it really you?"

"Juan, Juan Fedora," came the disbelieving reply. And then, peering more closely at Juan's companions, Don Sebastian recognized his very own nephew, Daniel Trigo.

Swiftly, the superficial burns were treated. Then came a flurry of explanations. The boys told their story first. The men listened closely, and then recounted their own tales.

"I have a confession to make," said Don Conta gravely. "I went after the reward for your capture, Daniel. Thank God, I didn't find you while in that frame of mind. Last night, returning home after a fruitless search, I deeply regretted what I'd done.

"Then, to make matters worse, I discovered that my Felipe was missing, I was sure that God had punished me for my wicked intentions. In the middle of the night, unable to fall asleep, I heard someone at the door. I prayed it was Felipe. I knew my actions had caused him great anguish.

"Instead, it was Don Sebastian from Madrid."

"My neighbor, David Trigo, has often spoken of you, in glowing terms," he added, turning to his visitor.

Don Sebastian smiled. "Let me take up the story. I was informed almost immediately that my dear brother and his wife had been taken prisoners of the church. I knew their only chance of ever being released rested with me. I am a financial advisor to the King and Queen.

"But it was not going to be simple. Lately, there have been

rumors of my own pending arrest as a secret Jew. My position was very precarious.

"So I approached the one Jewish man in Spain who wields almost limitless power, my good friend, Don Abraham Seneor, a Jewish rabbi and businessman. As we all know, he was largely instrumental in arranging the marriage of the royal couple more than twenty years ago.

"Don Seneor gladly intervened on my behalf. Before long he obtained papers ordering the release of David and Sarah Trigo.

"With the papers in hand, I spent two days travelling. Knowing the Conta family are trustworthy friends of my brother, I decided to come here first. Thank God, I made the right choice."

Don Conta flinched with guilt and gazed down at the floor. His son, Felipe, came over to him and held his hand, while Daniel gently told him that he had acted with true courage.

"Forgive me, Daniel," Don Conta murmured, meeting the boy's eyes.

Daniel smiled warmly. "There's nothing to forgive."

With a lump rapidly forming in his throat, he turned to his uncle. "How can I thank you, Uncle Sebastian?"

"Daniel, even though I am what is called a Marrano and was forced to change my name from Trigo to Santos, I am a loyal Jew. Your father and I are brothers, and will always be. I have done my duty and nothing more."

The next day, David and Sarah returned home. Daniel had been afraid for his parents, afraid of the lasting damages of Church torture. But they returned to him frail but healthy. It was Fray Deigo himself who, unwittingly, was responsible for their well-being.

The priest had all along assured his brethren that there was no hurry to begin the torture. There was plenty of time for suffering. He yearned to watch the Trigos tremble with fear, shake with indecision, grovel for mercy...or convert. In the end, they had escaped the fate he'd planned for them. The reunion of parents and son was joyful beyond words.

The family's happiness was marred only by the knowledge that they could no longer remain in their beloved Allerema. Without Sebastian's protection they were vulnerable to the malice of their enemies.

With sad farewells they left the home they loved and departed for Madrid, where they would live close to the Santos family. There was also the consolation that Juan, with whom Daniel had forged a wonderful friendship, would be there, too. On the surface, the Trigos could have no relationship with the Marranos whatsoever. Jews and so-called Christians stayed far apart. But spiritually — that was a different story.

Especially touching was Daniel's parting from his friends, the brave and fearless Pedro and, above all, loyal Felipe, whom Daniel called, "my Catholic brother."

The fire which had raged through the night had ended by razing the notorious abbey to the ground. Two charred bodies were discovered in the rubble. The bodies were assumed to be that of the keeper of the church, Father Ambrosio, and his esteemed colleague — one of the Inquisition's most effective interrogators — Fray Antonio Diego. The priest's fanatical campaign to condemn the Trigos had cost him his life.

The End

A Prisoner

Reality hit home. The chance to save Juan beckoned temptingly. But just moments before, he'd seen how futile it was for a bunch of children to even think they could free his parents. Now there were just the two of them.

Daniel's rebbe had taught that a person has to fend for himself — but only, of course, within the limits of the possible. Here, surely, the odds were stacked against them. Furthermore, failure meant grave danger to the Conta family who, as ardent Catholics, had little to fear otherwise from the Inquisition.

"Felipe, you cannot imagine how much I appreciate your desire to help. But it's no use. We two can't overcome the might of the Church. With God's help, my family will eventually be safe, and we'll all lead happy lives." Though his tone was optimistic, his heart was heavy.

Felipe was even smaller than Daniel. His body seemed to be

swallowed up by the rich, fertile hills of the Spanish country-side. "Daniel, you must not visit my house at any time," he choked. "Remember, my...my father is after the reward money for your capture..." His voice trailed off in a whisper.

Even though Daniel was saddened and angry about his father's neighbor betraying their friendship, he recalled the Torah's teaching not to judge others unless you've been in a similar situation. He swallowed hard, and then spoke in a level voice.

"Your father is a good man, Felipe. Times are bad. He must be hard pressed for money. Who knows, maybe I would do the same if I were in his shoes." He smiled. "Thank you for warning me."

He urged the boy to leave before first light. Felipe protested at first. But when Daniel insisted, his friend obeyed at last. With a last wave Felipe ran off into the hills. He didn't look back. Alone again, Daniel became suddenly conscious of the cold. The night air, seeping under his thin clothes, was slowly turning his skin to ice. All at once he felt an immense weariness.

"I must think," he told himself sternly, trying to shake off the wave of hopelessness that threatened to drown him. "There has to be a solution!"

His best option would be to reach Madrid and locate Uncle Sebastian. Oh, but he was so tired. Also, how was he to pay for such a long trip?

Despondently, he contemplated going back to his beloved home. At least he could rest there. Then he shook his head in the dark. That would be asking for trouble. The place was probably being watched day and night. Fray Diego would reason that the bird never strayed far from it's nest...

Eyes burning with fatigue, Daniel thought of digging a hole, jumping in, and somehow covering himself up. It was a bleak prospect. What he wanted most of all was to curl up in his own safe bed, and wake up to the smile of his mother, reassuring him that the family was safe and well. She would tell him that this whole horrible mess was just a nasty nightmare. Instead, with a sigh, he curled up under a gnarled old tree, huddled against the chill, and fell into a fitful sleep.

His slumber deepened as the hours wore on. He awoke with the sun shining full in his face. But the light in his eyes was only one of three things that startled him back into the waking world.

The second thing was the buzzing of flies. Attracted to his aching body, they were landing and taking off with irritating frequency. Still half-asleep, he waved them away as he drowsily recalled something Rabbi Kilmo had once said about flies. His rebbe had compared the tiny insects to the evil inclination. "No matter how much one tries to swat them, they invariably dodge the blows. Continuously dicing with death, they come back for more." Daniel tried to shoo away the pesky things, but they kept coming back for more.

The third reason was a strong feeling that he was being watched. Lying in the bright sunlight, he felt exposed and vulnerable. He had to get up, find a safer spot where he'd be hidden from prying eyes.

He stretched, blinked, and came fully awake.

Looming over him was the snarling face of Fray Antonio Diego.

The priest was accompanied by a short, stout man wearing the insignia of the Roman Catholic Church.

"Good morning, dear boy," said Fray Diego, in a voice smooth as honey. "How fortunate that you were able to arouse yourself from your peaceful repose. My heart would have broken at having to wake you and deprive a young child of his most precious beauty sleep."

His polite tone was somehow more sinister than the most

threatening shouts could have been. Daniel stared at him dumbly, too terrified to answer.

The priest's eyes narrowed. "But never fear," he snarled — the polite veneer gone now. "It won't be long before you'll be able to enjoy a long, long rest...a permanent rest...in the pit of hell!"

Before Daniel could stir, the two hooked their arms beneath his and pulled him roughly to his feet.

"There'll be no getting away this time," Fray Diego snarled, as the boy stumbled between them down a steep hill towards the abbey. Numbed as he was with fear, an ironic thought flashed through Daniel's mind. Only a few short hours ago he had been straining to think of a way to get inside that grim building. Now, here he was, being dragged into it. God, it seemed, had heard his prayers...

"Move!" mouthed the henchman. "Maybe a slap will get you to walk like a human being!" The flick of the man's fat, flat hand on his cheek sent a rush of anger through the boy. The anger brought with it a gleam of courage.

"I'll show them," he thought in a fury. Slowly and clearly, he began reciting aloud the declaration in Hebrew that every God-fearing Jew says upon opening his eyes in the morning. *"Modeh ani lefanecha..."* The words acknowledged that the Everlasting King had restored his life after his journey into the oblivion of sleep.

"What kind of witchcraft is this?" screamed Fray Diego. "Stop it, I say. Stop it, at once!"

Defiantly, Daniel retorted, "You're too late, priest. I've said it...and now you'd better watch out!"

Pulling Daniel with even more force, Fray Diego cursed and muttered. The three arrived minutes later at the doors of the abbey, where Daniel was thrown headlong inside. Like a rag doll he was dragged along a narrow corridor until they reached a locked room.

"There'll be no getting away this time," Fray Diego snarled.

"You and your friend from Madrid can bemoan your fates together," cried the friar. "I'll wager that within a week you'll both be dead...or else loyal Christians. Your choice is clear!" Bundled into the small room, Daniel gazed upon the proud, handsome features of Juan Fedora. The door slammed shut behind him.

Juan looked weary and pale, but otherwise unharmed. The two boys hugged each other and almost danced for joy at being reunited. Despite the deadly danger they were in, for the moment nothing mattered but that they were together again.

When the initial euphoria had died down, Juan described to Daniel how he'd been interrogated for a full day after being taken prisoner. Fray Diego had been careful not to hurt him too much, lest his injuries prevent him from furnishing the church with valuable information.

"Unfortunately, they managed to get out of me that I was from Madrid, but I have so far managed to withhold my name. When they find that out, my family will be doomed."

Somberly, Juan added that he had been informed in no uncertain terms that the Madrid authorities were investigating his identity. It was only a matter of time before they found what they were seeking.

Strangely, for the next three weeks, the boys were left mostly alone, though security was strengthened. Apparently the Church no longer underestimated the two lads. By standing on each other's shoulders, the boys were able to look out of a tiny barred window high up in their room. They saw many people patrolling the grounds of the abbey. Was there any way out of their prison?

After this period, the screws were tightened. They were separated and fresh interrogations began. For days the boys were given nothing to eat but water and stale bread. The only redeeming feature was that Fray Diego, who had shown such a lively interest in their case, was no longer in the abbey.

The new set of Inquisitors were not as harsh or single-minded as Diego. They seemed to doubt whether they'd get much valuable information from a couple of youngsters, and so were only going through the motions. They appeared content to allow Daniel and Juan to continue denying any involvement in acts against Church or country. Eventually, much to their delight, the boys were put together again.

Whenever they could muster the energy, the boys learned Torah together. It seemed doubly precious to them in this place, where they stood to lose so much. Being in prison brought home the importance of the mitzvot. The games that had consumed so much of their interest before their arrest no longer had any appeal.

One long afternoon, Juan told Daniel how he had come to rescue him outside the Meir house.

"At the time, I didn't tell you, because we needed to rest. Now, there is plenty of that available," he laughed wryly.

"Your Uncle Sebastian got word that your parents' arrest in Allerema was imminent. I remember him saying that he could intervene with the King and Queen, but preferred to use that option only as a last resort. It was better to get the family to Madrid where they could shelter under his protection. Those were his very words, Daniel.

"Because we are Marranos, I'd spent a great deal of time in your uncle's company. We had many secret learning sessions together delving into aspects of our *true* religion. After much thought, he decided it was safer sending a child to Allerema to warn your parents. Adult Marranos nowadays are forever being searched and asked questions. A boy would not attract such attention.

"He decided to send me without the knowledge of my parents, who would never have consented. I must admit he felt bad about doing that, but I was very excited and convinced him that only I could succeed. In the end, he justified his decision by the grave threat to the lives of your Trigo family.

"Anyway, I left immediately and arrived safely in Allerema. On my way to your house, I was told by a townsman that your parents had been arrested. I was too late! While I was trying to make up my mind what to do, I was stopped by priests. I convinced them I was a loyal Catholic — so much so, that a loose-tongued fellow bragged to me that they were on their way to the Meir house where they would trap you. He was sure you would make your way there, as you could not have known that your parents' friends had been taken into custody.

"I decided to hide close to the house and try to get to you first. The rest, of course, you know."

Three months later, Daniel and Juan were moved from the abbey. Their new prison was more like a reformatory for delinquent children. There they remained for six months, until March 31, 1492 — the date the order was given to expel all Jews from Spain.

They were given three days to leave. Daniel and his friend were thrown out the back door of their prison. There was no further use for them, sons of an exiled people.

Turn to page 104.

Home

It was a great idea, but how did Felipe propose to free Juan?

His Catholic neighbor was at a loss for words. "But we'll think of something," Felipe insisted. "The two of us can do it!"

Daniel had his doubts. Two youngsters, pitted against the might of the Church? "No," he said, shaking his head. "We'll never succeed on our own. There are too many of them, and they're too powerful."

"What do you propose, then?" Felipe asked, deflated.

"Let's get some adults to help us. It's our only chance."

Reluctantly, Felipe admitted that his friend's idea made sense. But adults were hard to come by. Whom to ask? And even more important, whom could they trust?

Daniel needed time to think and a haven to do it in.

A scene flashed into his mind. Close to his home was a wall of long, overhanging bushes. The umbrella-shaped greenery formed an alcove where a few boys could stand comfortably. Wistfully Daniel remembered happier times, when he and his friends would while away the long summer afternoons in their hideaway.

It would be dangerous being so close to his home. But on the other hand, who in his right mind would ever guess that a frightened young fugitive would take the risk of going back?

Felipe had no inkling of Daniel's hideout. The only boys Daniel had admitted inside had been Jews and Marranos. But times had changed. Now he was only too pleased to let his closest friend in on the secret.

"We'll stay there at night, if need be, while we plan our operation," Daniel suggested. "There are probably some things still left over from last summer, when we used to sleep out there."

Using the remaining hour of darkness, the boys quickly crossed the few miles to the Trigo house. Daniel found the hideout exactly the way it had been. Safely inside, the two crawled under a couple of blankets, and fell fast asleep without further ado. It was mid-morning when Daniel awoke. It was quiet inside the glade, and all was well with the world. He'd spent the night camping out with friends. Now, home for a scrumptious breakfast...But, wait, not so fast. Daniel awoke fully — and came down to earth with a thud. Swiftly he summed up his predicament. His parents were prisoners, probably already condemned to die. He was on the run, and doubtless destined for the same ill fate...

"Good morning, Daniel," said Felipe, appearing alongside his friend. He had been awake for a good two hours, but had waited patiently and with consideration for his friend to stir.

"Felipe! I had forgotten about you. Thank God you're here." Daniel meant every word. Difficult as his life was, it would have been a hundred times harder alone. His misery evaporated. "Come on," he exclaimed, jumping to his feet. "We've got some plans to make!"

First, though, Daniel excused himself for half an hour, while he davened the morning service. The tiny pocket-size siddur, from which he recited the prayers, was a permanent fixture in his shirt pocket. The boys munched on part of the store of dried fruit they'd found in the hideaway, while they tried to come up with names of people who could possibly help them.

All the while, they watched the house through tiny, narrow splits in the curtain of leaves. The place was still. There was no sign of suspicious activity. Tantalizingly, Daniel's beloved home beckoned to him. There was plenty of food there, and comfortable beds. But tempted as he was, the boy dared not venture out of hiding. For all he knew, lurking inside waiting to pounce were emissaries of the Roman Catholic Church.

Felipe was in the middle of a sentence when Daniel, his eye to a crack in the foliage, suddenly put out a hand. "Sssh," he hissed.

"What is it? What do you see?" Felipe tried to find another spy-hole in the hedge.

It was a carriage, pulling up outside the deserted house. As Daniel watched breathlessly, two hefty men came out of the house. So they had been waiting after all! The next few seconds became etched in his memory forever.

Alighting from the rear door of the carriage was the one person whom Daniel had least expected to see in the whole world. His very own mother, Sarah Trigo!

Stifling a cry, Daniel squinted in an effort to see better. His mother, walking slowly with a slight stoop, entered the house. The two hefty men stepped into the carriage. The horses bolted off at once, leaving a trail of dust in their wake. As suddenly as they had arrived, they were gone. All was totally silent once again. Daniel stared at the quiet house, shaking his head. Had he imagined the whole thing? A puzzled Felipe assured him that it really had happened.

"Daniel, your mother. She is in your house — didn't you see?"

"Yes, yes. I saw. She is alive! Come, we must go to her."

All his half-formed schemes were tossed aside. Daniel, body and soul, ached to be held in his mother's arms. Their separation had not been that long, but for him, it had seemed years.

"I'll go home," Felipe suggested tactfully. "I'll come back later." Daniel agreed, but for a different reason. "You are right. Who is to say that this isn't a plot to trap me? Go home, and please God, I'll make contact with you. It's safer that way."

The friends parted. Daniel crawled out of the bush, exposing himself to the world. It didn't matter anymore. To be with his mother was all that mattered to him at that moment. He walked up to the front door and gingerly opened it. Choking back tears, he called: "Mamma, Mamma!"

Sarah Trigo came out of the kitchen, her step still slow and awkward. "Daniel!" A glass of water she had been holding slipped from her hand. The crash of splintering glass echoed like the thunder of trumpets. Daniel ran headlong into the outstretched arms of his weeping mother.

As he melted in her embrace, he felt for a few precious seconds transformed back again into the little boy he'd been just a few days before.

"My baby! Oh, my baby!"

It was some time before mother or son could speak coherently. Soon, like the good Jewish mother she was, Sarah prepared her son a piping hot meal. While she worked she spoke of her imprisonment.

The most important news was that her husband, David, was alive and relatively well.

Detained in the castle from the outset, the pair had been constantly bombarded with questions. Coordinating the inquisition was Fray Diego, sitting mostly on the sidelines and occasionally taking notes.

Then, without any warning, Sarah continued, the priest

had come into their dungeon the day before, smiling broadly. He had apologized profusely for all the inconvenience the arrest had caused. It had all been a big mistake. Sarah was free to go.

Fray Diego had told David not to worry. He, too, would be released shortly. The holdup was due to a technicality which he did not explain. He also told Daniel's anxious parents that the search for their son had been called off.

After Daniel had taken in all the facts, he remained silent a moment. Then, he spoke.

"Mamma, I don't trust him. What he did isn't like him. It just doesn't make any sense! We have to find out what he's really up to."

Sarah didn't know what to say. Knowing who they were dealing with, she was inclined to agree with her son. But shouldn't she clutch at every ray of light? It was conceivable that the priest had had a change of heart. However, deep down she refused herself the comfort of relying on his words. The shock of betrayal would be too much for her to bear. She was still grappling for an answer when there came a knock on the door.

Daniel bravely stepped forward and opened it. On the doorstep was his friend Felipe. Behind him stood a familiar, hated figure. It was a tall, smiling priest. Fray Antonio Diego!

As he stepped aside, dazed, to let them pass inside, Daniel vowed he would not leave his mother again. In the Bible, Joseph stood in front of his mother, Rachel, to protect her from Esau. He would do the same for Sarah, his mother. He would be her protector.

If Fray Diego had come to exchange pleasantries, fine. But if he had a different, more sinister purpose, Daniel Trigo was ready for him.

Turn to page 110.

Kaddish

It was night, and the air was chilly. "We're free," Daniel muttered in astonishment to his friend, Juan Fedora. "What does it mean, Juan?"

"Expulsion — for you, my friend," Juan replied soberly. "It means that you have to leave Spain." He frowned. "For me, I'm not sure. As Marranos, we may have to stay."

Juan's voice became resolute. "Whatever happens, I've got to get back to Madrid and see my family. Come with me, Daniel. If your Uncle Sebastian is there, we could still save your parents."

"Do you think so?" a voice was heard out of the darkness. The boys spun around, groping like blind men in a strange place. "You didn't think I would let you off so easily, did you?"

Into view ambled the tall, gaunt form of Fray Antonio Diego. It had been a long time since he had crossed Daniel's path, but the evil of his presence had not diminished.

The priest was cloaked in a brown robe with a hood covering his head. In one hand, he held a long, wooden staff with a cross carved out at the top.

Instinctively Daniel tried to run, but his legs refused to obey him. He stumbled and almost fell. Juan gripped his arm, steadying his friend with a hand that was none too steady itself.

"Oh, don't bother to flee," the priest snapped. "I'm not going to hurt you poor little Jewish dears. I'm not even going to put you back in prison. You are both free to go."

Daniel found his voice. "W-we are?"

"The expulsion order pardons all who undermine the purity of our state — namely, Jews and Marranos alike. A stroke of fortune for you, don't you agree?"

Daniel had only one thing on his mind. "My parents! Are — are you saying that my mother and father are free to go?" he asked with baited breath.

"Poor, poor boy," Fray Diego chuckled. "I'm not saying that at all. For the simple reason, I'm afraid, that they were burnt at the stake — only hours before the decree was announced. What a shame, what a shame. Had they been alive today...I'm so sorry." The priest didn't sound sorry at all. Daniel, in his grief, threw himself at the robed figure and pounded his chest with his fists. "No, no, it's not true, you're lying!" he screamed hysterically.

Fray Diego was enjoying every minute. He gloated, watching the boy flailing his arms like a frenzied puppet while the priest stood in complete control. Catching the boy's wrists, he held them tight.

"You listen to me! For attacking a priest, I can have you killed in an instant — expulsion or no expulsion! But to tell the truth, it pleases me to see you go mad with grief, to see you pine for those whom you will see no more." He turned away, releasing Daniel's wrists with a flick of contempt. "Now, get out of my sight, both of you!"

As Daniel and Juan started stumbling away, the priest called out again. "Oh yes, Fedora. Do not consider *your* parents safe, either. We are fully aware they are practicing the Jewish faith. So to put you in the picture, you are correct when you say they will probably stay...forever. Don and Donna Fedora are prime candidates for the stake."

Daniel stood helpless against the mocking evil laughter of Fray Diego, but his Marrano friend was defiant as ever. "You won't get away with this. The hunter will become the hunted. For you, there will be no peace!" Juan predicted in anger.

"Why, you little...I ought to..." the blood was racing to the priest's head. In the nick of time, he controlled his temper. He was too old to let himself go like this. He could do himself harm if he were not careful.

"Say what you like, you dog!" he said in low-pitched fury. "The last laugh is with me. I hope you have a pleasant trip back to Madrid. Farewell!" And then he was gone.

Daniel Trigo slumped to the ground. His world had fallen apart. "I cannot carry on," he mumbled in despair. "There is nothing left to live for."

"Daniel, stop it! Stop it, at once!" Juan implored. "Do you think your parents — may God bless their souls — would have tolerated your speaking like this? I can imagine how you must feel, but you *must* carry on. You must live — for them, for your people!"

"Juan, I can't even say kaddish for them. We need ten Jews over the age of bar mitzvah for me to do that." Even this slim comfort was denied him. He broke into deep, shuddering sobs, and, without realizing it, did the right thing under the circumstances. He ripped the thin shirt he wore. Strangely, this action restored his will to live. He raised his head. Juan was right. Mamma and Poppa would have wanted him to carry on. He must persevere.

"That's better, Daniel," Juan said with approval. "You are

very brave." He placed a hand briefly on his young friend's shoulder, and then turned back to the road. His tone was decisive. "What we have to do now is get out of Allerema."

Despite the animosity towards the Jews, Daniel found he still had friends in his hometown. He also discovered that no one — including the Conta family — was aware of the fate which had befallen David and Sarah Trigo. Fray Diego must have arranged the execution in secret, Daniel concluded. His deep sorrow was swallowed in rage and bitterness. It was a heavy, heavy burden for such young shoulders to bear.

The loyal band that gathered around Daniel and Juan provided them with money, clothes and food for the trip to Madrid. The Contas offered to sell the Trigos' house for Daniel. They would make arrangements for the money from the sale to be forwarded to him before he left Spain.

"The house? I suppose there is no longer any need to keep it," he agreed, with a forlorn look in his eyes. Everything he loved and knew was moving out of his grasp, one by one. The tears that were never far away threatened to fall again. With steely resolve he held himself together.

Some days later, the two boys arrived in Madrid. Daniel's uncle Sebastian, Juan's parents told him, was away on a secret mission for the queen. But — to the boy's vast relief — he was expected back that very day.

As he waited impatiently to embrace his relative, someone of his own flesh and blood, Daniel kept busy by gathering ten Jewish males to recite the kaddish for his parents. He believed that each day that passed without his performing this important mitzvah would cause sadness to his parents in heaven.

The city was teeming with Jews preparing to leave. Daniel joined the adults for morning services in a large hall, which in happier times was used for festive occasions. Minutes before the kaddish prayer, as Daniel was gearing himself for that profound moment, a portly, well-dressed man charged into the synagogue. He was breathless and gasping, and it was plain to see he'd been running. Hard on his heels was a young girl of about twelve-years-old.

Panting, the man called out in the silence of the astonished congregation. "Daniel! Daniel Trigo, my nephew. Are you here?"

Daniel whirled around. "Uncle Sebastian. Oh, Uncle!" He ran into his uncle's arms, crying as if his heart had broken — as, indeed, it had.

Sebastian pushed him away, still holding the boy in a powerful grip by the shoulders. "Daniel, I have been told that you are saying kaddish for your parents!"

Sebastian was trembling with excitement and shouting at the top of his voice. The minyan circled around, perplexed and outraged at this interruption in the service. The young wisp of a girl with long, brown hair and fair, even features stepped forward.

"Daniel, this is Faiga Casimo. Tell him, tell Daniel the truth about his mother and father!"

In contrast to the outspoken Sebastian, the girl was shy and soft-spoken. But her voice came through, especially to Daniel, with the clarity and breathtaking splendor of an immaculately blown shofar. "Daniel, I was with your parents in prison. They are still alive!"

Gasps reverberated around the hall. The boy felt faint. Swaying, he was prevented from falling only by his uncle's hold on his shoulders. Somehow he managed to stay on feet as he listened to what the girl had to say.

Faiga Casimo told him that, amongst others, David and Sarah Trigo had indeed been sentenced to death. The announcement of the Expulsion had saved their lives.

Sebastian took up the story. "Faiga was released and came to Madrid. She told me that the friar was planning to kill my brother and his wife. They had been confined to a special prison. I had to work fast.

"I was fortunate in acquiring vital documents from Ferdinand and Isabella. Accompanied by two of their emissaries, I travelled with all possible speed to Allerema.

"It was not long before we met up with Fray Diego. He resisted furiously. His strength was of such a ferocious nature that I honestly believe he had it within his power to kill all of us.

"He was swinging wildly with a wooden cross when, all of a sudden, he collapsed in a heap. Blood spurted out from the holes in his face. It was grotesque. Apparently, in his fury, he'd burst a blood vessel. He died almost immediately.

"We were to learn that he had been furious at the reprieve that in his diabolical thirst for revenge, he had told you that your parents were dead. He wanted you to suffer in their place. He told you his lie only a couple of days before our arrival in Allerema. As it happened, we were actually in town at the same time.

"I returned here to Madrid — to hear that you were here, and seeking a minyan to say kaddish. Daniel, my dear boy, thank God it is unnecessary! Your mother and father arrive in Madrid later today."

And so it was. The family was reunited. Daniel thought he would never tire of embracing his mother and father, or gazing into their beloved faces or seeing their tearful smiles. It was the happiest day he'd ever known.

The family departed eventually for Italy. With them went Sebastian and his family, the Fedoras, and the girl, Faiga Casimo, who struck up such a lasting friendship with Daniel that they were married ten years later. The couple lived long, happy lives, full of mitzvot and good deeds, to the everlasting credit of their families and their people.

The End

Foiled!

As Daniel eyed him with suspicion, the priest graciously bowed to Felipe.

"Thank you for so kindly providing me with the wonderful
news that young Trigo happened to chance upon his mother.
Catholics like you are a great credit to society. I must remember
to reward your parents well for your services." Fray Diego
chuckled, and turned away. "You may go, young Conta."

Daniel knew that Felipe wanted to say something, but was
afraid. The troubled look in his eyes, though, spoke multitudes.
Daniel summoned a smile for his friend. "It's all right, Felipe.
Good-bye."

Reluctantly, Felipe left.

"Aah, such loyalty," said the friar, addressing himself to the
Trigos. "Daniel — that is your name, isn't it? I have already
apologized to your mother for the terrible inconvenience she
has had to put up with. Now, I must make my humble apologies

to you as well."

His voice grew harder. "Please understand, both of you, that we cannot leave any stone unturned in protecting the innocent flock of our religion who are susceptible to — how shall we say? — alien influences.

"Let me assure you that it is only a matter of time before Don Trigo will be able to join you. We just have to tie up certain formalities, that is all."

"What about Juan Fedora?" Daniel asked boldly.

"What about Juan Fedora?"

"Will he be released along with my father?"

"Why should he be?"

"He has done nothing wrong!"

Fray Diego opened his mouth in mock amazement. "Little boy, with all due respect, were you yourself not witness to his blatant and malicious assault on two loyal Catholics — one a priest, no less?"

"He was acting in self-defense," Daniel retorted hotly.

The priest's manner turned cold. "Are you accusing good people of wrongdoing and, at the same time, calling me a liar?"

"No," came the quick reply. "You said that the arrest of my family was a misunderstanding. This fight was also based on a misunderstanding. Those two men believed that Juan was an enemy, and attacked him. There was nothing wrong in their actions, just as there was nothing wrong in what Juan did."

"Hmm. You are a bright child, clever beyond your years. Only answer me one thing: Why are you interested in the acquittal of this boy from Madrid? He is no longer a Jew!"

The ever-so-slight pause indicated Daniel's quandary. To betray his friend's Marrano leanings was unthinkable. But what other explanation could he give for his concern?

To his rescue came his mother.

"Oh, Father, how can you ask such a question?" Sarah asked softly. "The Fedoras used to live in Allerema. Daniel and

Juan are only two years apart in age. The older boy spent much of his time playing with our Daniel. He was like an older brother to my son. Remember, Daniel is an only child."

"Oh, that explains it then. I am much obliged, Señora, for the information." The Spanish priest bowed sardonically. A loud knock interrupted his next words.

"Excuse me," murmured Sarah, worried. She opened the door, wondering what new unpleasantness lay in store.

She was almost bowled over as a group of finely-dressed soldiers barged past her into the house. They were resplendent in their red tunics, large green berets and white, single-striped navy-blue pants tucked into shiny, knee-high boots. They bore the mark of proud members of the elite Royal Guard.

The leader let out in a booming voice: "Make way, make way for the emissary of the King and Queen of Spain, His Excellency Archbishop D'Angelo!"

The soldiers moved aside to form lines on opposite sides, heralding the entry of an extremely short, elderly, grey-bearded man with a twinkle in his eye. Shrugging off the fanfare, the man shuffled in. "Not necessary boys, totally unnecessary," he commented.

He turned to the Trigos and Fray Diego and heaved an exaggerated sigh. "Oh my. I'm no military man. All this fuss and bother, you know, I don't know what it's all for. I'm just a simple priest — no time for pomp and ceremony."

"Who are you, sir?" inquired Fray Diego, singularly unimpressed by the newcomer's comical antics.

"Who, me? That's a good question, Father. One thing for sure, I'm no 'sir.' Just an old man. In fact, I'm a priest, like yourself."

"Yes, I can tell that from your clothes, even though your behavior would have me think otherwise," Fray Diego said tartly.

"Aha, a man of wit, I see. Still, I shall ignore your remarks. Far be it for me to criticize a fellow cleric. To get down to business, I'm seeking a certain Fray Antonio Diego. Perchance you know of his whereabouts?"

The friar winced slightly. "Who wants him, may I ask?"

"Can't see any harm in telling," beamed the Archbishop. "The King and Queen, to be precise. I have an important message for him, and was told he can be found in this very house. That's why I am here."

A message from the Crown. Fray Diego assumed an air of humility. "I am indeed the man you are looking for. And you are...uh, I cannot quite recall what the soldiers said?"

"D'Angelo, Father D'Angelo — this Archbishop tag is mostly for show. Pleased to meet you. My instructions are to inform you that King Ferdinand urgently requires your presence in Madrid. He has a most important business matter which only you can handle properly."

"I see." Fray Diego sounded gratified. "This, I must say, is most unexpected. But before I depart, you understand, Your Excellency, I have unfinished business to complete here." He pointed to Sarah and Daniel, who had been standing silently to one side. The friar threw them a smile which reeked of evil intent.

"I am sorry, Father." The Archbishop was terse. "I am to take over your affairs here until your return. There can be no delay. You must leave immediately."

Once again,the priest's manner underwent a change. "How is it that I have never heard of you?" he asked, peering more closely at the older man. "I am familiar with all of the King's close circle. Also, what type of an Archbishop mocks his station? Something here smells very wrong."

"Oh no, you are mistaken. Nothing smells, Father — except your future, if you ignore the Royal command."

"Where are your orders?" Fray Diego demanded. "I want to see them!"

"My orders? Of course," replied Father D'Angelo.

On a signal from the Archbishop, two soldiers broke out of

line. In one swift movement they seized the friar's arms, pinning them behind his back. Fray Diego was unable to move. The short man produced a long dagger from underneath his frock. Deftly, he swished it to and fro. With amazing speed and dexterity, he jabbed the sharp point into the craggy flesh of the priest's throat, stopping just short of the protruding blood-red line of the jugular vein.

"These are my orders!" he snapped, his voice quite different now from the indolent Archbishop's. "Take us to the castle, where you will instruct the guards to bring you David Trigo."

Eyes bulging with fear, Fray Diego spluttered back, "What makes you think I'll do it?"

The so-called Archbishop D'Angelo said, "If you value your life, you will obey."

"What happens to me afterwards?"

"A good question. Afterwards, we'll take a stroll to free a second good soul...and then, well, it's up to you."

"What do you mean by that?"

"I mean that if you're a good boy and behave yourself, we'll set you free. If not..." The words trailed off meaningfully.

The dagger inched a fraction deeper into the pulpy skin of the priest's neck, producing a tiny, bubbly speck of blood.

Events after that moved quickly. The transformation of Fray Diego into a subservient lackey was a wonder to behold. He performed his task admirably. Cool as a cucumber, the mysterious Archbishop D'Angelo and his cohorts accompanied the priest to the castle where a surprised David Trigo was promptly released. He was whisked away into the waiting arms of Sarah and Daniel.

Fray Diego's ploy was at an end. As Daniel had suspected, he had only freed Sarah in order to flush her son out into the open. But the temptation to engage mother and son in a match of wits had proved his downfall. The delay enabled "Archbishop D'Angelo" to reach him at a most opportune moment, alone with the two Trigos. The threat of imminent death posed by the valiant band of rescuers prevented the friar from thinking of ways to signal to his loyal troops that he was being forced to speak at dagger's point. By the time David Trigo was released and they were outside again, the moment had passed, and it was too late.

The priest's misery was not yet over. Fray Diego was also forced to set free Juan Fedora. It was then that his mind snapped. He could take no more of this humiliation. Struggling like a wildcat, Fray Diego attempted to break free from the clutches of his enemies. With almost superhuman strength, he lashed out at the soldiers surrounding him. In the ensuing melee, he ran headlong into the pointed spear held by one of the guards. The metal penetrated his heart. Fray Diego died instantly.

There were no witnesses other than the "Archbishop" and his band of followers. Hastily, they buried him in the forest.

In actuality, "Archbishop D'Angelo" was no more a member of the clergy than Daniel was. His real name was Michel Domingo, Spain's foremost stage actor, who was a close friend of Daniel's Uncle Sebastian. The influential Marrano had recruited his services and that of his loyal troupe of actors. The priestly garb was merely a disguise to trick the friar into releasing his captives. Michel and his cast returned to the Royal Palace to entertain the King and Queen, without anyone being the wiser as to their brave exploits on behalf of the Jews.

In the meantime, the Trigos fled to Madrid where they lived under the protective wing of Sebastian. Juan Fedora was reunited with his family.

In the space of a few days, Daniel's childhood had come to a premature end. But his experiences toughened him and deepened his faith. They also helped him to face the trials that beset him and his people during the Jewish Expulsion from the shores of Spain a few months later...but that's another story.

The End

Indoctrination

From a state of stunned confusion, Daniel's mind suddenly became crystal-clear. He would bow to the Cardinal's authority. He would go along with him, and await his chance to regain his freedom. The boy's sudden answer rang out, loud and clear. "Your Excellency, I want to accompany you to Seville to seek the truth."

Raising a bushy eyebrow in surprise, the Cardinal at first seemed unsure how to react. And then, with an authoritative raising of his fist, he roared, "I knew it! Indeed, a wise choice!"

To the hushed crowd, he bellowed, "Well, aren't you going to say something? Can't you see that the lad has shown great courage? He deserves your support!" It was an order more than a suggestion.

"Hurray! Hurray!" the crowd responded dutifully, but in a dull, muted fashion.

"Aaah," the Cardinal nodded. "Methinks you folks are disappointed that the boy did not choose the way of his mother and father. You hard-working people are called from your well-deserved rest to ensure that our country is purged from evil corruption. But do not worry, my good folk. The wheat must be separated from the chaff. It may well be that young Daniel Trigo will pass the test and become one of us.

"On the other hand," the Cardinal continued, raising his voice for dramatic effect, "if he fails — simply put, he will lose his head. For rejecting the truth, he will deserve death."

No Jewish blood was spilled that day. The disappointed crowd sauntered home in droves past the young boy, muttering and yawning. Placing a chubby, bejewelled hand on Daniel's shoulder, Cardinal Bialo escorted him to the carriage.

No sooner had the stark, market scene faded into the distance, when a satchel lying on the seat was scooped up by the priest. He pulled out a shiny, black book with a silver cross emblazoned in the center of the leather-bound cover. This he thrust at Daniel. "Here. Familiarize yourself with the contents of the Holy Book. In a very short while, you will be as accustomed to its wisdom as any pious, Catholic boy your age."

Daniel watched his own hand shaking and could do nothing about it. He took the book gingerly, as if at any moment a snake would spring out from between the covers. The Cardinal was observing him closely. Feigning genuine interest, Daniel opened to the first page.

The title, "Bible, New Testament," shot up at him. He longed to close his eyes, to blot out the hateful words. But he had no choice. He had to read on.

Struggling valiantly to keep his head from nodding sleepily, he sat out the ride without daring to lift his eyes from the pages. The Cardinal's presence loomed large and silent next to him.

Finally, upon arrival in Seville, the boy was separated from the man who had plucked him out of the bloodthirsty crowd. He was taken to a low-level building adjoining what appeared to be a sprawling mansion. He was soon to learn that these quarters were an annex of a magnificent cathedral. Its opulent trappings were befitting the place of worship of a leading luminary of the Church. The Cardinal's own complex of living quarters, offices and — it was rumored — torture-chambers, was built into a maze of corridors adjoining the cathedral.

Daniel found himself alone in a small, bleak room. For company there was a wooden crucifix hanging on the wall and the ever-present Bible. A lighted candle and a rickety bed were the only other furnishings.

For two days he saw no one. "Aren't they going to do anything with me?" he wondered in growing dismay. These hours of waiting for who knew what horrible fate was the worst period Daniel had gone through during his whole ordeal.

He got his answer on the third day. It was then that the programming began in earnest. The Jewish youngster was subjected to a rigid routine of indoctrination, starting before the sun rose and lasting well into the night. No effort was spared to fill Daniel's mind with the stories, doctrines, laws and beliefs of the Catholic religion. Physically, he underwent the motions of attending church services, the occasional vows of silence, midnight mass, and solitary introspection. Two expert tutors were assigned to serve his needs twenty-four hours a day.

Food was sparse. There was little opportunity for sleep. From the outset, Daniel was determined to maintain the Jewishness within himself. He began with the Sabbath. "I was taught that I must break its laws if necessary, to stay alive, but at least I'll know when it comes and feel its sanctity," he consoled himself.

But the subjugation took its toll. By the fourth week, Daniel was racked with confusion. Was he Jewish? The life which had formed him gradually receded into a dream-like world. After months of constant brainwashing, the past was almost erased from his memory.

Daniel found himself alone in a small, bleak room.

They called him Christopher. He began to believe that his entire life had been spent in service of the Church. Ironically, he was compared to the boy Samuel of the Old Testament who, after he was weaned, was donated to the Temple by his grateful mother, Hannah.

"You are today's Samuel, dear Christopher," he was told encouragingly. "One day you will make a great priest, maybe even a pope!"

Gradually, the harsh programming wound down. More and more time was spent with the Cardinal. Daniel's face, emaciated and haggard after the first phase of conversion, began to sparkle with a fresh, invigorated zest.

Food was now plentiful. Carefully selected areas of travel were mapped out. The new Christopher had long ago been moved from his first stark little room into the main building. There he occupied a room right beside Cardinal Bialo himself. He began to pray with fervor. A flourish of faith swept over him, like the soothing surge of warm water washing over a frozen body. For all intents and purposes, Daniel was no longer Daniel. He was a fully fledged Catholic.

It was at this precise point when those who had molded him made a fateful mistake. Convinced that his transformation was complete, they permitted a certain priest, Fray Antonio Diego, to pay his respects to the budding child prodigy.

"Good day, young Christopher. Your fame has spread far and wide in the realm, dear boy."

Inexplicably, the convert shivered with nervousness. "What for, Father? I have done nothing to warrant fame."

"Aah, such superb modesty! Always a good trait, I assure you. No, my young man. You are mistaken. In today's modern world, very few souls are absolutely dedicated servants of the Church. Young people prefer to taste the decadence of forbidden fruits. But you...I congratulate you."

"Thank you, Father. You're very kind, but it's not necessary. I am perfectly happy with my lot."

"Good, very good! Now, I have to go. I may be back again for another visit. If, of course, it pleases you."

The priest shook his hand in friendship. The boy found it difficult to return the warm sentiments. Limply, he let the priest hold his hand. The old man's palm was surprisingly fleshy for such a thin-boned form. Their eyes locked.

Something in the man's long stare triggered a strangely uncomfortable feeling in the boy. He had seen the priest before. Somewhere, in a vastly different world...

The friar finally spoke. "I have lingered long enough. Goodbye, my boy — for now." Fray Diego turned away.

Was it coincidence that the very next day Christopher received yet another visitor? After months of persistant clamorings to see the boy, Don Conta was granted his request. "It's the least we can do," reasoned the Cardinal. "He was instrumental in the boy's capture, after all."

The man who had been a neighbor of the Trigos for many years did not come, however, to take pride in his actions. Rather, he was full of remorse for betraying the Jewish family. Long ago he had decided to make amends by helping the prisoner escape from the cathedral.

If he had not come so soon after Fray Diego's visit, Daniel (or Christopher) would have scoffed at his urgings to flee. In hushed tones, the man spoke fast and furiously. Daniel listened, scarcely breathing, to the entire story of who he was and what had befallen him and his family.

Slowly, the memory of his past seeped back. Shivering with fear and bewilderment, Daniel broke out of the cocoon which had infected his mind.

"Daniel Trigo. Daniel Trigo. My name is Daniel, not Christopher. Fray Diego. The bushes. Watching. I...I saw them being threatened...for being Jewish. I am a Jew." His voice broke. "MAMMA, POPPA! I remember, I remember everything. Oh, Don

Conta!" Recognizing his neighbor again, Daniel clasped him with all his might. Beads of perspiration, both clammy and warm, trickled down his forehead and chest. "How could I have been so stupid?" he sobbed. "How did I let them do this to me?"

"It was beyond your control," Don Conta said comfortingly. "But we have to be quiet. If somebody hears us, his suspicions will be aroused immediately."

"I must get out of this place. I must, Don Conta!"

"Don't worry. I got you into this mess. I'll get you out. Just have a little patience — and faith in your God."

The next day, Daniel escaped.

He had gone with a pair of priests to a nearby parish. On the way, their attention was diverted by a wagon blocking the road. While they were involved in an altercation with the wagon driver, Daniel, unattended, slipped away to the waiting Don Conta hiding behind a tree. It was easy. Nobody expected Christopher to even contemplate straying from his companions.

Nobody — except for Fray Diego. The way the boy had looked at him before he left had continued to haunt the priest. How much did he remember? By the time he rushed back to the Cardinal late the next day, warning him to lock Daniel up and throw away the key, the boy had already vanished. He was too late.

"I'll get him. I'll get him, if it's the last thing I do," he vowed, gritting his teeth in rage and frustration.

Daniel emerged from his luxurious prison only days before the Edict came to expel the Jews. In a short while, he would be swept into exile along with thousands of others of his faith.

Turn to page 133.

Not to Cry

D aniel stood very still. He did not know what to do.

Of the choices available to him, the worst possible fate was the Cardinal's offer. How could he willingly expose himself to the false teachings of the Church?

But to remain openly defiant was no answer either. "If I tell them I remain loyal to my religion, I am afraid they will kill me — and I don't want to die," he thought to himself.

Cardinal Bialo strained his ears in mock anticipation of the boy's decision. An ugly mood descended on the square. The people stirred restlessly, filling the air with angry murmurs. With each passing minute the crowd resembled more and more a bloodthirsty mob. Sensing the shifting mood, Daniel roused himself to speak. His voice sounded frightened in his own ears. "I — I think I would like to be alone for a while before deciding."

"Speak up boy!" someone shouted. "Let us all hear what you have to say!"

"Remember," said the Cardinal, "you owe justice to these fine, upright people who have stayed up all night to pay their respects to our glorious Church!"

Making fun of a boy in abject fear of his life was much more to the crowd's liking. Now, they began to vent their pent-up energy by laughing and jeering, like an audience beguiled by clowns at a circus.

The Cardinal mocked along with all the rest. "So you want to be alone, do you, boy? Need time to think? Answer, Trigo!"

Was this really happening? Daniel felt numb. "Yes," he stammered. "I want to be alone."

"What?" shouted the priest. "Louder! Let us all hear what you have to say. Louder!"

A cry of anguish flew from Daniel's lips. Then, suddenly, he screamed out for all to hear, "I NEED TIME TO THINK. YOU SAID I COULD BE ALONE AND THINK!"

"Aha," Cardinal Bialo nodded gloatingly. "You do have a voice. Good. Alright, you may be alone. We won't bother you." He turned to face the muttering crowd. "Everybody remain dead quiet. You heard his request — he wants to be alone. So be it. If we do not speak, it will be like being alone."

Raucous laughter echoed around the square, until the Cardinal motioned for silence. An eerie stillness fell over the square.

It was broken by an occasional cough, a snigger or two, people putting fingers to lips with a mocking "Shh!"

Daniel stood alone. Valiantly he fought his tears. He couldn't cry. When he was much younger he'd shed childish tears for not getting his own way. More recently, he sometimes wept when he was hurt.

"But not now!" he told himself fiercely. Then he shouted it aloud. "Not now! Not for me!"

The crowd was perplexed. What was the boy saying?

"I shall not be humiliated," Daniel said in a low but carrying voice.

"I shall not be humiliated," Daniel said in a low but carrying voice.

All at once he felt stronger. He understood the game that the Cardinal and his mob were playing with him. They had no intention of letting him slip away unharmed. Well, if that's what they wanted, he would beat them at their own game. He would shed his childish image and become a man before his time. He would not cry. Daniel conjured up in his mind the picture of his father and mother smiling proudly at him. Somewhere they were alive. He concentrated on the image, willing himself with all his might to believe.

"They are giving me the strength to carry on. Thank God, they instilled in me a simple faith that the Almighty controls the world. Never has my faith been so strong. For the first time, I do not fear these people." In this vein Daniel prayed silently. The crowd began to show a greater restlessness. Although his thoughts had only taken a few seconds, they were more than enough for the weary men and women who waited in the cool night air. "What's taking so long?" a gruff voice shouted from the back. He was quickly shushed; the Cardinal had not lifted his order of silence. But the spirit of the mob was clearly in accord with the shouter.

Daniel looked up. Spiritually uplifted, he was prepared to defy the masses and pronounce his allegiance to the God of his forefathers. Doing so would in all probability precipitate an attack by the mob, ending in his own death. He hesitated, agonizing.

"There has to be some way I can get out of this alive and still be Jewish." He *had* to stay alive, for while there was life, there was hope — hope not only for himself, but for his beloved parents. He gritted his teeth and resolved to accompany the Cardinal. He would step into the Catholic trap, but he would not succumb. With God's help, he would persevere.

Turn to page 116.

The Crazy One

awn crept over the village. Outlines became clearer. The noise grew louder. Cardinal Bialo's bloated face was clearly visible to Daniel now, smooth as silk. The skin looked too young to shave. Or was the Cardinal's face powdered?

Strange thoughts to flit through a boy's mind at such a perilous moment. And strange, too, that Daniel felt no fear. He wondered why it was that the sky, turning blue amid the fading stars, had never looked so beautiful to him before. The rich green of myrtle trees ringing the square were a feast for his eyes. Even the drab clothing of the crowd of peasants had their place. The square throbbed with life, and he wanted to be part of it.

Daniel was under no illusion. If he openly declared his love for the God of his people he would not be spared the wrath of the Catholics. The precious gift of life — gone!

And yet, he was filled with a strange new exhilaration. Dying in the name of his God — the one true God — was the ultimate sacrifice. In doing so, he would earn an eternal reward greater than any he could possibly imagine.

"I am a Jew — now and for all eternity!" His voice rang out clear and loud, for all to hear.

The silence that followed his words seemed deafening. Shivering uncontrollably, Daniel braced himself. The crowd would go wild now, surging for the young heretic, mad for his blood...He closed his eyes, waiting.

But things did not go quite the way he'd expected. His stirring simple words, spoken with such pure and honest resolve, tugged at the heart-strings of even the most rabid anti-Semites in the crowd. The silence stretched as the peasants shuffled their feet, uncertain.

The Cardinal turned to face the crowd, his voice confident and bland. "I have no doubt the boy is quite sincere in his beliefs, my friends," he said. "It shows just how far the vile Jews have succeeded in indoctrinating their young ones in their mistaken beliefs.

"However, as I've said before, we are a just nation. I have decided that the boy be placed in a special institution where he will receive treatment for his...condition." He paused. The crowd hung breathlessly onto his every word. "It may very well be that, like others, Trigo is beyond hope. However, he is a bright lad. I think perhaps his tainted soul can still be saved."

The crowd erupted in hoarse cheers at the wisdom of their leader. When the cheers died, the mood of the mob changed. The peasants became suddenly aware of their own weariness. It was almost dawn, and they wanted their beds. The Cardinal nodded his head benevolently, and they took this as their cue to trudge off to their homes. With sleepy murmurs they began to move away.

Daniel stood dumbfounded. He couldn't believe his good

fortune. What a narrow escape! He was not free, but neither had he been put to an early and horrible death. He was left alone with the Cardinal and his men. His ultimate fate remained hidden — but he was alive. He was alive!

The peasants had almost faded from view when, without any warning, a shrill scream sounded. It penetrated the square like a trumpet blast. At the noise, the multitude of pigeons perched on walltops, and spread out like a sprawling carpet over the pebbled square, flapped their wings in a panic and literally leaped with fright. There was a great rush as they took wing overhead. The peasants stopped in their tracks, looking around in bewilderment.

Again the scream came, clearer this time.

"Shema Yisrael!" The voice belonged an old woman.

"The Crazy One," the peasants muttered, crossing themselves. "It is the Crazy One."

Dressed in a simple black frock, with a black scarf covering her sparse white hair, the old woman hobbled quickly up to the pedestal where Daniel and the Cardinal stood frozen. Eyes blazing, she pointed a long, bony finger at Daniel.

"God bless the Jew. The boy shames you all!"

Stunned out of their drowsiness, the peasants began to come back. Their murmurs grew louder. A ripple of excitement passed through the crowd. Tension began to mount.

"The Crazy One has gone completely mad!"

"She is a witch!"

"No, worse — she is a Jew!"

Her name was Donna Isabella de la Torre. It was well-known that once upon a time — many, many years before — she had been the matriarch of an established Marrano family. Her love for Spain and the Church had gradually become a legend in the town. When the present Queen rose to the throne in 1468, she had even adopted the royal name: Isabella.

By that time, people had stopped taking her seriously. A

series of tragedies had wiped out her family, one by one. It was after the death of her only surviving grandson that she was given her nickname. He had been killed at a lavish "auto-da-fe," a great outdoor gathering at which he was burnt at the stake on suspicion of secretly reverting to the Jewish practices of his ancestors.

In public, the "Crazy One" still clung to the Catholic belief. Her piercing "Shema Yisrael," the age-old cry of Jews everywhere, caused great shock among the townspeople. "The Crazy One is a Jew!"

Daniel, too, became caught up in the confusion. The old woman's plaintive cry moved him deeply. But on a different, more practical level, he knew he was once again in very great danger.

Quite suddenly, she was beside him on the platform. He saw her stark gaze, her face wild, haggard. A few yellow stubs in withered gums were all that remained of her teeth. She must have been well over a hundred-years-old.

"Run, my angel. Go, like the wind," she screamed. "Don't let them take you!" The townsfolk shouted and began closing in on the boy. One more time he glanced at the old woman. Her eyes blazed like a fiery volcano as she willed him with all her heart to flee.

Frantic, Daniel swung around. On one side a gap had not yet been closed. With a mighty jump, he catapulted himself off the pedestal, lost his footing, regained his balance, and was off as quickly as he could, while favoring his injured leg.

Even as he ran with his heart pounding in his ears, he couldn't fail to hear a last, high-pitched shriek of laughter. The mocking cry was the last sound the "Crazy One" ever made. While Daniel sped off towards the maze of avenues branching away from the square, the angry horde descended on Donna Isabella de la Torre, determined to silence her for all time. But the old woman cheated them of their aim. In that instant her soul passed peacefully from this life, before a single hand could be laid on her. All her life, her devotion to the Church had been a complete pretence. The "Crazy One" had, in fact, inspired a family of Marranos to hold secretly fast to its Jewishness.

For the rest of the day Daniel lay low in a pitted trench not far from the square. Tired and hungry, he emerged at midnight to try and find some food. Once again, what seemed to be nothing more than mere chance occurred at that moment, but what happened would forever change the boy's destiny.

Coming up fast behind him were three men. Furtively, he moved behind a pillar. He stood dead still, fists clenched in fear, waiting and watching.

The men's voices, sounding more than slightly drunk, echoed in the still of the night. Despite the slurred speech, he had no difficulty in making out who they were discussing: the "Crazy One."

"There I was, all ready to string her up for the vultures," one of the trio related in a thick, petulant tone, "when this old fellow comes along. He had two men with him. Before any of us could make a move, he picked up the Crazy One, put the body in a carriage, and just took off." He shook his head. "I tell you, I was all set to throttle him."

"Didn't you do anything?" his crony asked.

"Sure I did. I yelled after him. The carriage stopped, and out he climbed. 'Hey, give me back that rottin' carcass!' I said. Then I saw his face. He had the look of the devil, I tell you." The speaker crossed himself. "I sure wasn't going near him."

"Who was he?" wondered the third man.

The speaker crossed himself once more, shaking his head once again. "I heard later that they headed towards the Jew cemetery. Like I said, the old man was either the devil, or a Jew...or both."

Daniel listened, scarcely breathing. As soon as the drunkards staggered off, the boy set off across town. "I must pay my respects to that old lady," he thought. "She saved me from that Cardinal...and who knows what else. I'll just look for a freshly-dug grave." He walked quickly, ears pricked for any sound that might spell danger and discovery. "I wonder who that man was, the one who took the old woman away to be buried?"

It wasn't long before he reached the cemetery. It seemed deserted. There was no moon, and the night was very dark. fighting down his fear, Daniel walked slowly amongst the graves. He passed row after row of simple stones, with the names of Jewish folk starkly engraved on their flat, smooth surfaces. The names seemed somehow to shine in the dark. He felt comforted to be amongst his own people at last. Physically, they had long departed, but Daniel felt some calm and comfort return here, among their final resting-places. "I am not alone. I am surrounded by wonderful people who are with their Maker."

Without realizing it, he came to the end of the last row. Suddenly, he bumped into a tall man. He stepped back with a stifled cry. The man was standing erect and looking straight at him.

Frightened almost out of his wits, the boy glanced upwards at the stranger's face. Before he could get a good look, the man stooped slightly, grasped Daniel by the arms, and lifted him up as easily as if he was picking up a few stones. Daniel went limp in his arms.

He was at eye-level now, and finally saw the man's face. It was hard as granite, bearded and strong, and yet the eyes were soft and gentle. Daniel had seen him before. He had met this man together with his father, and had never forgotten the experience.

Holding him like putty was — in his father's words — the greatest sage of the generation. Rabbi Isaac Abravanel.

Turn to page 142.

Bar Mitzbah

The Edict decreed by King Ferdinand and Queen Isa-bella was signed in the city of Granada on March 31, 1492. The reason given for the expulsion of Jews was to prevent them from inflicting further injury upon the Christian religion.

For twelve years, steps had been taken to curb the Jewish influence. Jews were forced to live in crowded ghettos. The Inquisition was established to root out heretics, and almost all the Jews were expelled from Andalusia, the area where Daniel grew up.

According to the authorities, their measures had failed. They now believed that expulsion was the final solution. The plan called for all the Jews to leave the country three months after the date of the Edict.

Daniel escaped from the hands of the Church only to find the country in turmoil. One piece of good fortune was that the search for the boy "Christopher" — which would otherwise have continued until his capture — ended almost at once. For the Church, there were more important issues just then. The smooth execution of the royal couple's orders, and saving souls by converting as many Jews as possible in the little time available — those became top priorities.

Don Conta, his loyal family friend, didn't want to take any chances. He hid with Daniel for two days in the cellar of an old, abandoned house. From there he ventured out cautiously, bringing the boy food from his own household. And then, quite suddenly, the expulsion order came. Only then did the two dare to emerge from their refuge.

Seville, not that far from Allerema, was abuzz with nervous excitement. Jews who had lived secret, furtive lives for years came out into the open. Daniel latched onto one of those families, who had also been good friends of his parents. He and Don Conta bid each other a warm if hasty farewell.

"Not only did you save my life," Daniel said seriously, "you also saved my soul. If it wasn't for you, I would not be part of what is going on today. I was becoming a Christian, a boy called Christopher." He gave his rescuer a tremulous smile and held out his hand. "May God bless you and your family."

Don Conta grasped the offered hand and pressed it warmly. "My next task is to help find your parents and reunite the Trigo family," he said.

"Oh, if only they're still alive!"

"I'm sure they are, Daniel. I don't have any proof, other than a feeling in my bones. And the situation being as it is now, with the coming expulsion, the chances are they will soon be released."

The boy took comfort from the Righteous Gentile's words.

However, frantic efforts to discover the whereabouts of the Trigos met with scant success. Word had come out of Allerema that Fray Diego had left to take up a position elsewhere. Daniel wanted with all his heart to return to his hometown, but this was no simple matter. Jews everywhere in Spain were making for the coast, where they could pick up boats leaving for Portugal — one of the few countries willing to take in some of the hundreds of thousands of refugees. Those travelling in other directions were apt to be hauled in for interrogation by officials who suspected the Jews of planning to stay in the country.

Despite the danger, Daniel was determined to go back home. He set about preparing for the trip. But when he was nearly ready to depart, he was befriended by an elderly rabbi. Pesach Luria had learned with Spain's greatest sage, Rabbi Isaac Abravanel, who was the leading figure bringing the Jews out of Spain.

"You cannot go back to Allerema, young Daniel," Rabbi Luria said sadly. "From what you have told me, too many enemies may be waiting for you there. In any event, it is more than likely your parents are somewhere else. There has been great upheaval in the prisons and people are being moved all over the place."

"I know that, Rabbi," Daniel said. "But...I just don't know where else to turn!" All his anguish and loneliness were written clearly on the youngster's face.

"Come with me to Portugal," the rabbi urged. "We will learn Torah on the way — and that, my dear boy, will auger well for the future of your mother and father."

Daniel studied the rabbi. The aged eyes were soft and kind-looking beneath a wide, noble brow. They radiated a glow of humility. A curly white beard half hid the rabbi's encouraging smile.

As if deliberately trying to avoid making a decision, Daniel posed an unusual question. "Rabbi, why is it you kept your beard? Everybody knows that it is a mark of the Jews. We have been persecuted for so long, wouldn't it be better not to have one?"

"You are right, Daniel. Life has been dangerous for our people. I lay no blame on any man who dispensed with his beard. But as for me, I wished to display my faith in the proudest manner possible." For a moment a frown darkened his brow. "The Jews have been tormented by the Church, forced to convert, exiled from their homes. I cannot tolerate giving in to their evil! I have deliberately kept my beard."

Daniel thought briefly before speaking. "I shall come with you, Rabbi. I know God will bring my parents back."

Rabbi Luria smiled warmly and nodded. He had never longed for the glory of a congregation or a large following. His strength was in his personal, kindly manner. Laying a hand on the boy's shoulder, the rabbi assured Daniel that if only one saw the ways of God in their rightful context, then the whole scheme of things could be understood.

"Do not fear. We will be safe. Your parents, too." Daniel was comforted. The old *talmid chacham* reminded him more and more of his own beloved rebbe, Efraim Kilmo, who was no longer in this world.

The exodus took on many forms. Some of the stories were sad. There were those exiles unable to pay passage money to shipowners. Others sought refuge in lands where they were mercilessly turned away. For some, uprooting an entire life was more than they could bear. After endless wanderings, these unfortunates returned to face the hardships of the Inquisition. Some Jews, who for years and years had stood fast against the Spanish Church, lost their strength of resistance and, alas, succumbed to Christianity.

But the failures were in the minority. The vast multitudes left on foot, in carriages, or in boats. The most striking feature was the manner of their departure. A notorious priest, who was no friend of the Jews, could not help but remark at the way he observed their parting:

"With hymns on their lips, each man helping and encouraging his fellow, and firm in their naive belief that the sea would divide for them as it had divided for their forefathers when they left Egypt."

By the 9th day of the Hebrew month of Av, the last Jew left Spain, save only for those who had fallen by the wayside, physically or spiritually. This was the date when terrible calamities had befallen the Jewish people throughout history — the most tragic being the destruction of both Holy Temples in earlier times.

Daniel and his new-found mentor secured passage to nearby Portugal. When they arrived, they joined thousands of other Jews in setting up temporary dwellings near the Portuguese capital of Lisbon.

Rabbi Luria, skilled in the trade, repaired shoes. He also taught Torah, mostly to children. To the little ones he brought to life the *aleph-bet*, while he introduced the beauties of *mishnayos* and *chumash* to older children. In Spain, the vast majority of the Jews had been spiritually starved. Now, the sage was greatly sought after for his wisdom. He refused all payment for his teaching.

His most cherished pupil was Daniel Trigo. They lived together, ate together, and learnt Torah together whenever the old rabbi had time. Daniel even watched him repair shoes, and in time acquired the skill himself.

Nevertheless, times were hard. finding money to support their families posed a serious problem for the Jews. Many found work in Lisbon, where they contributed their skills to the local populace. The Jewish refugees gave also freely to each other, creating a spirit of togetherness.

The Jewish quarter in Lisbon not only provided homes for the Jews who had been forced to leave Spain, but also served as a meeting point for Jews on their way to other pastures. There was a constant activity of coming and going in this vibrant community, where so many were crammed into so small an area.

His most cherished pupil was Daniel Trigo.

After a few months, the Portuguese grew fidgety with this thriving alien culture in their midst. Their initial acceptance of the refugees now turned into discontent. It looked like a second Jewish expulsion would not be long in coming.

Before another six months had elapsed, many of the Jews were leaving again — this time for North Africa. Among these were Rabbi Luria and his pupil. But before their departure a milestone in Daniel's life was to pass. His bar mitzvah.

The depth of knowledge Daniel had gained from his teacher, Rabbi Luria, was well-known in the community. But even without that distinction, Daniel was well-liked by his fellow Jews. Kind, and sensitive beyond his years, he endeared himself to all he met.

The morning of his bar mitzvah fell just a week before Daniel's departure for Casablanca, Morocco. A huge crowd gathered in the makeshift, central synagogue for the Monday morning reading of the Torah. A gay mood held sway when Daniel was called up to recite the blessing and the portion of the week. He rose with great joy, to become for the first time a member of the ten-man minyan.

A man of distinguished bearing was among the congregation. He had arrived from Spain the previous evening on his way to Morocco. He had been informed that a bar mitzvah was to be celebrated and was impressed by the wonderful turnout. When the *gabbai* called out Daniel's name for him to take center stage, the man started incredulously. A cold chill ran up his spine. Had his ears deceived him? No, no, it couldn't be. It was a figment of his imagination. He was hearing things. Obviously, the name belonged to someone else...

He saw the small, slight frame of the bar mitzvah boy step up to the *bimah*. A fierce cry strained to erupt from his lips, and a flood of tears poured down his cheeks. No one in the gathering heard his soft exclamation: "Daniel, my son! Daniel!"

Standing unknown and unheralded at the bar mitzvah of his own son, David Trigo would not, or could not, interrupt the solemn moment. When the final *brachah* was concluded, he moved forward through the congregation and stood opposite the boy.

Daniel's eyes widened. His head began to spin, and a strange buzzing sound filled his ears. For an instant, he almost fainted. Was he dreaming?

The other worshippers realized that something was afoot. A wave of emotion radiated from the pair on the podium and affected every person there. The story of the dramatic reunion began to circulate through the synagogue. A great surge of applause rose up. People who were privileged to witness the scene said afterward they had never been so touched in their entire lives as when father and son hugged one another after almost two years of separation, during which the boy had believed his father to be dead.

David took Daniel to his mother, Sarah, at the other end of the Jewish quarter. Gently, the boy revealed himself. It was the happiest moment of her life. When last she'd seen him he'd been no more than a small boy. Now, although still slender and wiry, he was as tall as she.

After the initial joy subsided, the Trigos told their story.

About three weeks before the expulsion order, they had been transferred to a prison in the far north of the country, where other Jews were held. A couple of months later they were released.

"Fray Diego was strongly opposed to letting us go," Daniel's father said soberly, "but he soon disappeared. Rumor had it that he had been killed by his own people, who — even by their standards — found his methods of persecution to go beyond human limits." He shook his head, as if to erase the memory of that cruel churchman. "Let us not speak of him again. After being freed, we had only one goal — to find you. We moved heaven and earth to gain information about your fate, but all our efforts were futile — we got nowhere. Our time had run out. Along with so many others, we were swept along with the tide and found ourselves heading for Morocco, by way of Portugal.

"Our hearts were bursting with grief. We believed that we would never see you — our darling only son — again. We could only pray that you were alive."

At this point Sarah spoke up. "Oh, my boy, I refused to give up hope. I don't know how — call it a mother's intuition — but I was convinced you were alive and well."

The family's prayers were answered. Together with Rabbi Luria, whom they couldn't thank enough for all he had done for their son, the Trigos travelled to Morocco where a new life awaited. In time Daniel Trigo became a great rabbi in his own right, and a revered family patriarch for generations to come.

The End

In the Shadow of a Sage

abbi!" was about as much as Daniel could gasp.

The man set him down with care. "What are you doing here so late at night?" he asked quietly.

Daniel struggled to catch his breath. "An — old lady — was buried here — today. She died to sanctify God's name. I've come to pay my respects."

"What is your name?"

"Daniel Trigo."

The man frowned. "Trigo? I've heard that name before."

"My father and I once travelled to Granada to see you. He had an important question to ask...I remember that the rabbi blessed me..."

"Do you remember your father's question?"

"Yes, Rabbi. My father wanted to know whether we should become Marranos. He used to say that if we stayed Jews, they would put us into prison."

"And do you remember what I answered?"

Daniel nodded in the dark. "The rabbi said we should remain true to our Jewish faith."

"Daniel," the man asked in a worried voice, "where are your parents?"

"They were taken prisoner a few days ago." Daniel fought the sudden tears that welled up in his eyes. "I...I managed to escape..." The great man began to pace the ground beside the boy, thinking deeply. After a moment he stopped abruptly, and picked up a shovel lying next to him. "Time to do a mitzvah," he said. "Here, take this and come with me."

A few meters away was a freshly-dug grave. "The lady lying here is Donna de la Torre. Is she the one to whom you wish to pay your respects?"

"Yes, Rabbi. Were — were you the one who brought her here?"

Rabbi Abravanel nodded soberly. "There was no other choice. She is a Jewish soul." He stuck the shovel into the soft soil, digging up a clump of grass and sand. Then with a mighty heave, he guided the earth onto the loosely-covered mound. When he was done he stood silently, gazing down at the new grave. "May she rest in peace. She was a righteous woman. She suffered greatly in her lifetime," the rabbi said in a low voice.

"People called her the 'Crazy One,' " commented the boy.

"She was far from crazy, Daniel. Only very, very old. She travelled far and wide to restore people's souls to Judaism. It was extremely dangerous. That's why she pretended to be a little...off-balance."

Soberly Daniel replied, "Today, she saved *my* soul. They wanted me to become a Christian and she stopped them."

The rabbi stood quietly. Both were filled with their own thoughts. Daniel was the first to speak his out aloud. "Oh, Rabbi, will you help me see my parents again?"

The moment Daniel had told him of his father's question,

Rabbi Abravanel had resolved to do all he could to help the family. "Of course, my boy. It is my privilege to make the effort of redeeming Jews who have been captured. It is one of the most important mitzvot one can do."

"I knew God would answer my prayers," Daniel whispered joyfully. And then, with enthusiasm, "When do we start?"

Rabbi Abravanel chuckled. "Not so fast, my young man. First, we have to make plans. Perhaps you had better fill me in on the details of their capture. With God's help, we will come up with something."

With a last look at Donna de la Torre's resting-place, Daniel followed the rabbi to a carriage which was partially hidden from view. The big man removed from inside a pair of tefillin and a large tallis.

"The sun has already risen, Daniel. This is an appropriate time to pray, but we have to leave the cemetery first."

Daniel, who had never been to a funeral in his young life, was puzzled.

"Jews are forbidden to stir jealousy amongst the departed," the rabbi explained, "by doing mitzvot in their presence that they can no longer do."

"But — they are dead!" Daniel protested. "They can't do them anyway!"

"True. Yet a part of the soul remains at the place of burial. For us to flaunt the mitzvot in this place would be in poor taste." Wrapped in a flowing white tallis, the Sage swayed and prayed to his Maker for nearly an hour. Daniel took hold of his trusty siddur and followed suit. He was finished well before his famous companion.

During the course of the morning Daniel accompanied Rabbi Abravanel on his rounds, collecting farm taxes on behalf of the King. They travelled together in the sleek but modest-looking carriage, driven by a competent driver also in the service of the royal couple. The boy asked the rabbi something that he'd been curious about: how he had retrieved Donna de la Torre's body.

"Where did the Rabbi know her from?"

"Aah, on my travels I meet all kinds of people — especially Jews, or those unfortunate souls who are Jewish at heart. Whenever I was in this area, I made a point of visiting her."

Daniel pondered a moment. He then asked what was uppermost in his thoughts. "Why is it that the Rabbi is not arrested for being Jewish?"

The sage smiled. "You ask so many questions Daniel — a true Jewish trait." He turned serious. "Believe me, I, too, have had to walk a tightrope. A few years ago I escaped from Portugal after being wrongly charged as a conspirator to bring down the ruling government. I will not burden you with all the details.

"Since then, God deemed it fit that I curry favor with the Spanish king and queen. The Almighty has endowed me with vast sums of money. I use my wealth in business transactions for the Crown, and have built up a steady relationship with Ferdinand and Isabella as a result."

Daniel had heard of the rabbi's remarkable influence. His outstanding modesty prevented him from mentioning his great personal popularity. He felt honored at the chance he had to spend time with this wonderful Jew.

Daniel was so absorbed in the rabbi's every word that he'd nearly forgotten their purpose in being together. A remark, out of the blue sent his hopes soaring. "My plan, Daniel," the rabbi said quietly, "is to use the powers in my possession to free your parents." The great Rabbi Abravanel was going to intervene on his behalf!

Exactly how was he to do it? Daniel had no idea, but he wasn't worried. The *tzaddik* and renowned scholar surely had his methods. David and Sarah Trigo would soon be safe. He was sure of it.

For the rest of the day, the rabbi was involved in his business affairs. Daniel marvelled at the respect that the

Catholics accorded the rabbi. For a man who collected money, he was incredibly well-liked.

Uncannily, Rabbi Abravanel seemed to read Daniel's thoughts. He smiled at the boy. "God wants me to succeed in these endeavors for reasons known only to Him.

"We are living in stressful times. In the not-so-distant future, we may all know why each of us had to go through our own particular experiences. Remember, though, to continue learning Torah and doing the mitzvot. Those are the actions which count and will eventually bring about our salvation."

That night, true to his word, the rabbi immersed himself in Torah. Sharing a room in an inn on the outskirts of the town, Daniel basked in the holiness by simply observing him learning. In the dim flicker of candlelight, the sage was absorbed in writing a commentary on the Book of Joshua.

As the evening wore on, he looked up from his work and noticed Daniel dozing. Gently, he placed a finger on his shoulder. Daniel jerked awake. The rabbi beckoned him to move closer. For the next half-hour they studied *mishnayos* together, before Daniel eased into a peaceful slumber. By the time he awoke a little after dawn, Rabbi Abravanel was already deep into his morning prayer.

As soon as he had finished he issued instructions. Daniel was to stay behind in the inn, while the rabbi made a few inquiries in town.

Daniel waited in a fever of impatience as the minutes crawled past. One hour went by, then another. The door opened suddenly and Rabbi Abravanel walked in, wearing a broad smile. "I've found them!" he told the boy. "Come with me!"

Daniel did not wait for a second invitation. Forgetting himself, he bounded toward the carriage, ahead of his distinguished friend. Sheepishly, he remembered his manners. He turned and apologized profusely. Rabbi Abravanel smiled, proud that the youngster had caught himself so quickly. Daniel hadn't meant any disrespect, he knew. The boy was just too exuberant to wait — and with good reason!

Events after that moved so quickly that Daniel was hardly able to recall them later. Rabbi Abravanel had a seal from the king and queen. With the seal in hand, the two of them had no trouble gaining access to the sinister prison where the Trigos were being held. Only one obstacle barred their way: Fray Antonio Diego.

Returning from an interrogation, the friar almost stormed headlong into the man and boy. He stopped short. He recognized both of them immediately. His surprise at seeing the rabbi was swept aside by his utter amazement at the sight of Daniel Trigo.

"Trigo — *you!*" He gathered his wits with lightning speed, and took rapid stock of the situation. Almost in the same breath he exclaimed with polite sarcasm, "Ah, the esteemed Rabbi from the Court of our gracious King and Queen. How nice to see you. I assume you are handing the boy over to me. The charges against him and his parents are serious indeed."

"No, Father," Rabbi Abravanel said firmly. "In fact, you have orders to hand over this boy's parents — to ME."

Fray Diego's face turned white. "What do you mean? They are prisoners of the Crown! Common criminals! On whose authority do you make these ridiculous claims?"

"On the authority vested in me by the King and Queen." The rabbi produced the royal seal.

Fray Diego clenched his fists in fury. At that moment he wanted nothing more than to hurl a dagger at Rabbi Abravanel, who threatened to thwart one of his most cherished desires — destroying the Trigos. His lips began to tremble, and he felt the blood rise to his head. He and the rabbi were of the same height. They glared at each other, eye to eye.

The priest broke first. Cowering before the formidable rabbi, he growled, "Take them. They are yours. But let me warn you, Rabbi. One of these days, Spain will rid itself of all Jews — including people like you, sitting high and mighty on your rich throne."

Even as the priest spoke he realized the folly of his words. As a man with ambitions of his own, he had to be careful not to make unnecessary enemies — especially powerful ones. He hastened to backtrack.

"I apologize for the harshness of my words, dear Rabbi," Fray Diego said with a forced smile. "A momentary lapse, that is all."

The rabbi did not bother to reply.

With Fray Diego out of the way, wheels were swiftly set in motion for the Trigos' release. Before long — thanks to Rabbi Abravanel and the loyal people who helped him — Daniel was reunited with his parents.

A year later, the paths of the great sage and the Trigo family would cross again, during the days of the Expulsion. But before then, Daniel revelled in the presence of his beloved parents. David, Sarah and their son spent many long evenings recounting tales of their adventures, and thanking the one true God for preserving them and bringing them back together again in joy.

As for Fray Diego, his own cruel nature proved his undoing.

Word trickled up to the evil Torquemada, the Inquisitor General, that the friar's over-zealous torture had caused ripples of dissatisfaction amongst the upper echelons of the government (information subtly supplied by Rabbi Abravanel). Torquemada decided to withdraw Fray Diego from his post — temporarily. The Church could always make use of his services again, later.

But that opportunity never came. Only weeks after Torquemada's decision, Fray Diego met his end. In the remote monastery to which he had retired, the friar was bitten by a snake — and perished.

The End

Message of Hope

The carriage rumbled along. Every so often, Count Rodriguez would flip open an eye to cast a glance at the young wanderer. Out of deference to the Count's slumber, an uneasy quiet filled the carriage during the rest of the trip. The miles rolled past as Daniel fought off the urge to sleep. He must stay awake, and alert.

So it was a bleary-eyed Daniel who felt a sudden tinge of excitement when the farmer exclaimed at last, "Look, there on the horizon — Madrid!"

The Count sprang to life and became instantly and fully awake. Daniel's eyes darted in his direction.

"What are you looking at, boy?" Count Rodriguez demanded. "Do you think I'm off to wallow in the lap of luxury? Well, you're wrong. I'm going to battle. Even though our victory against the Moors is imminent, my presence is still required at the front." He smirked. "Essential, in fact."

The Count continued his bragging, and Daniel had no option but to listen. "I am a general — and a strategic genius, if I do say so myself. Almost single-handedly I have wreaked havoc on the Arab hordes...But what concerns me now is your future." There was little time for the boy to absorb the meaning behind the count's last sentence, for the horses had finally slowed to a halt. Awaiting their arrival were soldiers of the Royal Guard. Daniel stood to one side, forlorn and alone, while the count huddled in earnest conversation with the troops. The way they were looking at him left little doubt that he was the main topic of their talk.

In the meantime, the lady who had paid his fare conferred with a pair of tall, burly young men. The carriage's other passenger, the farmer, had hoped to stay around and see some fun at Daniel's expense. But unable to find a suitable excuse for lingering, he reluctantly walked away.

One of the two young men drew the Count aside in idle chatter. At the same time, the second man casually sidled up to Daniel and thrust a piece of paper into his hand. The man stared intently at him for a few seconds with pale, blue eyes, and then rapidly backed away.

Daniel shook off his confusion and peered down at the scrap of paper. It contained a message:

Fear not. Help is on the way. Shema Yisrael.

At that moment the Count came striding towards with him, flanked by the soldiers. Heart pounding, Daniel dropped the paper to the ground and quickly covered it with his foot.

"Jump into the carriage, boy," the Count ordered. "You're going for a little ride!"

Daniel, bewildered, swung his head around in instinctive appeal to the lady and the two young men, but they were nowhere to be seen. Without his noticing they had vanished.

There was no one to help him. He was trapped. What lay in store for him? The Count would surely make good on his threat to discover who he was. Then he would be hanged ...Never to see his family again...Wait. What about the strange, cryptic note? The man who had given it to him must have known he was Jewish. It was the lady who wrote it — of that he was certain!

The elegant, cobbled streets of Madrid whizzed by. Gradually the carriage moved into an area of upper-class villas, with their majestic pillars up front and, like a pair of sentinels, two long windows with open shutters on either side of the thick oak doors. Then the neighborhood changed. Affluence gave way to squalor and filth. Now the carriage was rattling along narrow dirty streets lined with little hut-like hovels. Young and old stood barefoot on the stony roadside, hungry and in rags. The horses cantered through the muddy, pock-marked lanes, pulling the carriage and Daniel towards a mysterious destination.

At long last, they stopped outside what seemed to be a large industrial building. Daniel was pushed roughly inside and thrown into a huge, dormitory-type room. It was empty, save for about thirty stinking mattresses scattered across the broken-tiled floor. A tremendous noise, like the smashing of iron, came to his ears from a different part of the building.

Something brushed his feet, almost knocking him over. To Daniel's disgust a giant rat, the size of a kitten, glared up at him. He felt he was going to be sick.

"Don't mind them," chortled the man who had brought him into the room. "In this place you'll find them your only friends. I'd advise you to rest a while. You'll need it. Tomorrow, you begin work — like the rest of them." Grinning wickedly, he threw the boy a mock-salute and sauntered out of the room.

As he had predicted, Count Rodriguez was called off to the front in the war against the Moors. He had been intrigued by the boy and fully intended to find out more about him on his return. But it was not to be. The Count was killed on the very day he set foot in Granada. Ironically, it was not the enemy who killed him, but a disgruntled personal servant gone berserk.

Daniel, left behind in the workhouse, became an anonymous number. Together with a number of boys and girls plucked out of a nearby orphanage, he worked day and night in the armaments factory that stood beside the dormitory. The factory produced swords, shields and spears for the war effort. The pounding and grinding of metal grated on the young workers' ears, causing partial deafness among many of them. Besides fetching and carrying, Daniel had to hold down sheets of metal as fearsome-looking artisans hammered away at the sharp surfaces to create weapons of various shapes and sizes.

Escape was impossible. Guards were posted everywhere to deter any thoughts of breaking out. Even had an escape route been available, the children were too weak to take advantage of it. All their energies were channelled into hard labor. With nothing but thin gruel to fill their stomachs, they were always hungry. They were permitted to sleep only a few hours a night, so they were always dead tired. They lived the lives of slaves.

Months passed. Daniel was completely cut off from the outside world — except for hearing about one event which should have affected the slaves directly. On January 2, 1492, Granada was captured. The last Arab stronghold had been broken. Spain was now one country. The Royal Court was set up in the war-ravaged city. One might have expected a slackening of weapons production, but the factory's grueling schedule continued unchanged. The days churned into nights. More months went by.

Forgotten was the message of hope. Almost, but not quite forgotten, too, was Daniel's original purpose in coming to Madrid in the first place — to find his Uncle Sebastian. Daniel clung desperately to the last of his strength. One by one the children fell, succumbing to diseases or — on occasions — to insanity. He prayed every night, trying with all his might just to remember, to recall his Judaism, to think of his parents. He was growing weaker by the day. Much longer, and he would end the way so many others had ended.

July, 1492. A young man by the name of Pancho de Seville had been searching for Daniel for some months. That summer he finally succeeded in tracking him down. To Daniel's shock, Pancho managed to have him released from the factory workhouse. The promise of help that Daniel had received so many months before was at last fulfilled. It had been Pancho who had handed Daniel the message from his mother, Anne de Seville.

Pancho brought Daniel to a safe-house some miles away. During the next weeks, the boy was nursed back to health. As his strength came flowing back, so did his memories. Where were his parents? How to resume his search for his uncle? But he didn't have the energy to think about his problems yet. He had to take one day at a time now, to become the boy he had been before all the recent horror had happened to him. Then he would decide what to do.

One day, as Daniel sat up in bed enjoying a bowl of hearty soup, Pancho decided that the time had come. Somberly he broke the staggering news:

"Daniel, it grieves me to tell you that the Jews have been expelled from Spain. They have all gone — my mother and only brother as well — to other countries, some on the other side of the world. I alone am left of the de Sevilles. I am a Marrano. You are a fugitive. The Church is after our blood. For the present, we are safe in this hideout, but if we tarry too long, our lives will be in great danger."

Daniel was shocked. "Jews...expelled?" he gasped. "My parents! What has happened to them?"

Pancho did not know, but he had more to add. "Listen

carefully. An Italian explorer by the name of Christopher Columbus sails from Spain in less than a week. This could be our last chance. I can get a berth on board for both of us, as sailors. You're young, but not too young. You can work."

"Yes," Daniel grimaced, as the memory of the hated factory rose before his eyes. "I can work."

"I strongly feel, Daniel, for your own safety, that you should come with me," Pancho urged. "I've definitely decided to go."

What Should Daniel Do?

Choice 1

Agree to Pancho's plan. Turn to page 168.

Choice 2

Say no, on the slight chance that he can make progress in his quest to find his parents. Turn to page 173.

22

ᎦᏰᏒ ᏦᎧᏣᏣᎬᏒᏕ ᎧᎸ ᏖᎻᎬ ᎷᎧᏌᏁᏖᎪᎥᏁᏕ

The Count's mocking words echoed in Daniel's ears. The farmer licked his lips and scowled, never taking his eyes off the boy. The lady did not pose a threat — in fact, she was Daniel's only hope of support. But how could she protect him against two thugs?

He made up his mind quickly. He had to give up this method of getting to Madrid. The way things looked, the odds were stacked against his reaching his Uncle Sebastian. Somehow he had to escape from the speeding carriage. It was not going to be easy.

The only way was to fling open the doors and jump. He'd have to wait for the carriage to slow down. There was a risk he'd be injured. The passengers would doubtless shout to the driver to stop the carriage. And even if he did manage to get away, where would he go? Here he was, in the middle of flat, expansive countryside, with the nearest town probably well beyond walking distance.

But it seemed he had no other choice.

About an hour or so later, the carriage began to climb a steep incline. The land had become mountainous. The horses slowed almost to a crawl. Daniel's pulse raced as his moment neared.

The carriage swayed from side to side. Just as he was bracing himself to leap towards the door and throw himself out, the carriage suddenly stopped in its tracks. The horses reared up on their hind legs and neighed with fright.

"What's the trouble, driver," screamed Count Rodriguez, rudely awakened by the sudden jolt.

"No trouble, Your Excellency," answered a soft but determined voice from outside. "Just a quick stop to pay dues to us poor folk." The door swung open, to reveal a youngish man wearing a black beret and moustache. He was smiling. A single gold earring dangled from his ear. Behind him were others on horses. The forlorn figure of the driver stood on the side of the road.

A long, gleaming sword swished teasingly under the noses of the passengers. "Smells delightful, doesn't it?" the stranger mocked. "I'm sure you all want to keep a healthy distance, eh? Sometimes I could swear that the infernal blade has a life of its own." He swept the sword lightly in a half-circle. The farmer cringed. The man with the earring glanced at the Count. "You're a man familiar with the church, Your Excellency. Perhaps, deep down my sword has a soul?"

"Be off with you!" snarled the Count. "You don't frighten me. I am a military man and have made mincemeat out of the likes of you. Now, I order you and your pack of scoundrels to step back. We wish to continue our journey."

The man with the sword bowed. "Of course, Your Excellency...after we conduct a little business." The playful smile vanished and the man's tone grew stern. "Out of the carriage — all of you!" The Count resisted, but he was no match for the band of men who dragged him unceremoniously out into the heat of the midday sun.

"Hand over all your valuables, and fast," the leader commanded. "We have no time to dawdle."

Surrounded by sword-bearing robbers, the passengers did as they were told. Coins, jewellery, and watches were produced.

Daniel, too, emptied his pockets. They contained nothing but a ragged lining. The head robber snapped, "Well, boy, out with it. You cannot fool me. Where did you hide the money?"

"I'm sorry, sir," Daniel stammered. "I don't have any."

"Don't play around with me. You could never have been riding this coach without money." The man moved ominously closer, grasping the hilt of his sword. "Now tell me, where is it?"

"Sh-she paid for my fare, sir," Daniel pointed. "This kind lady."

The man stared at the woman. She had given up her valuables without protest. She nodded, looking the robber chief straight in the eye. Very slowly she said, "Yes, it is true. We found the boy on the road. I took pity on him and paid for his ticket to Madrid."

"I see." The robber looked pensive. "If you are not telling the truth, Madame, it will go very ill with you! I shall come to Madrid and skin your hide myself. But," his glance flickered to the other passengers, "if these others verify your story..."

The Count spoke up gruffly. "Yes, she is a fool. We almost trampled him underfoot. Pity we didn't. You can leave him be. I am taking him to Madrid, where he'll be placed under my supervision. He will be taken care of, I assure you."

The man said thoughtfully, "If that's the case, then I'm sorry to disappoint you, Your Excellency. We can do with an extra pair of hands ourselves. The boy stays with us."

"Why, that's kidnapping. You'll never get away with it!"

"That's enough from you. Get back in now," ordered the

"Hand over all your valuables, and fast," the leader commanded.

robber, gesturing roughly with his sword. "We have no further need of you."

Boulders, which had been set up in the narrow pass to stop the carriage, were rolled away by the robbers. The passengers — except Daniel — were bundled back into the compartment. The Count was gnashing his teeth in fury and swearing revenge; the farmer cowered in fear of his life; the lady resumed her silent stance. The driver snapped his whip over the horses' heads and, with a rumble, the carriage wheels began to roll. The last Daniel saw of it was a cloud of dust rising from the dust-filled road.

Daniel's six-month sojourn amongst the famed "Robbers of the Mountains" had begun.

He soon learned, to his surprise, that the band of men were far more than just robbers.

"We are Christians, Jews, Moors and Marranos," the chief robber told him as they ate a simple meal by campfire that night. "You might say we are political freedom-fighters who use the guise of robbers to ward off the Church." The robber reached for a stick to poke up the fire. "Why am I telling you all this?" he continued, though the boy had not said a word. "Because I am a Marrano. That distinguished lady in the carriage happened to be my mother, Anne de Seville. My name is Michel. I have two brothers in Madrid who await her return."

Daniel was flabbergasted. "I can't believe it! My name is Daniel Trigo. I am a Jew."

Michel did not seem surprised by the admission. "My mother would not have bought a ticket for you unless she had a reason. She is a very astute lady. Remember how slowly and clearly she spoke to me? That was her way of confirming that you were one of us, so to speak."

The ways of God were indeed mysterious. Even though they had gotten wind that Anne was a passenger on this particular trip, the outlaws had decided to rob the carriage anyway. "If we become too successful, the whole country will be on our trail. Therefore, we choose our targets carefully." He smiled ruefully. "I don't know whether I have endangered our operation by robbing someone like the Count, but I had a burning desire to see my mother again. Just think — if I hadn't, you wouldn't be here."

Fortunately, there were no direct repercussions from the authorities. Daniel began a new life beneath the stars of central Spain. It was the life of a Jew. He prayed, learnt and endeavored to do as many mitzvot as he could.

On occasion, the placid routine was drastically shaken by a robbery. Daniel preferred not to accompany the group on such escapades and his request was always granted.

As to the fate of his parents, Michel encouraged the boy to bide his time. "Right now, the political climate is very volatile, which would hamper any negotiations for their release. Let's wait, Daniel. Something is bound to happen."

And it did. Victory against the Moors triggered off the expulsion of the Jews. The camp was thrown into a state of uncertainty. The Jewish robbers did not know which way to turn. Most left the hideout and returned to their homes. That was Michel's intention, too — but he decided to wait for a while. His own identity had been known for some months and he was afraid that he would be immediately arrested upon arrival in one of the cities. Daniel stayed with him.

At last, Michel deemed it safe to leave. He and Daniel travelled to Madrid. The de Seville family had joined a mass exodus to Portugal. Only one son, Pancho, had remained behind, awaiting his brother. The resemblance between the two was striking.

"Michel!"

"Pancho!"

The brothers embraced. Daniel stood shyly to one side until

Michel introduced him. Pancho shook his hand warmly. The three sat down to plan their future.

"It is not too late to reach the family in Portugal," Pancho said. "Ships are leaving regularly, despite the fact that the deadline for the Jews has already passed."

Michel discussed his options into the early hours of the morning. He decided finally, to leave at once for Portugal. But for Pancho and Daniel, there was another way out. Pancho revealed some interesting news. The explorer, Christopher Columbus, was leaving shortly on a long sea voyage, to find a route to the Indies.

"I can get us on board," said Pancho, a gleam of excitement in his dark eyes.

Daniel hesitated. He did not want to leave Spain permanently. If he did so he would probably never see his parents again. But the spirit of adventure was upon him. Bidding farewell to Michel, he joined forces with the second brother, Pancho.

Turn to page 168.

Beneath the Veil

The little boy craned his neck to peer out of the window. The Spanish countryside whisked by, dotted with flourishing fruit trees in full bloom. Count Rodriguez's snoring almost matched in volume the din made by the constant rattling and pounding of hooves, vibrating loudly in the confined space of the carriage.

As the miles grew between himself and Fray Diego, Daniel's fear lessened. He let himself relax. Slowly, the monotonous rumble of wheels on hard gravel lulled him into semi-sleep.

From time to time the bouncing of the carriage jolted him awake, and his mind raced anxiously. How to make secret contact with the woman? There was no way he could pass her a message without alerting the others. Little did he know that, at that very moment, a pair of big blue eyes were peering out at him from behind the veil...

A sudden jolt woke Daniel with a start. The carriage

seemed to leap over a small boulder in the middle of the road, rousing the passengers and causing a buzz of consternation among them.

"What's happening?" growled the Count.

"It was nothing, Your Excellency — just a bump," said the farmer. "Don't worry, I haven't been sleeping. I don't trust this brat one little bit. There's no telling what he might do if we're asleep and off our guard. I've heard tell of vicious robber bands wandering about these parts..."

Even as the farmer spoke, the carriage pulled to a halt. The driver, alighting from his perch above, opened the carriage door and poked his head inside. He apologized for any inconvenience, and guaranteed nothing like this would happen again. "We were coming around a bend. I had no time to brake," he explained.

"Well, don't go so fast next time, you imbecile!" the Count roared. The driver saluted obediently, and resumed his station.

Now that he was awake, Count Rodriguez decided to eat. From under his seat he produced a large satchel full of meaty delicacies. Following his example, the farmer, too, began to gorge himself on an array of pork sausages, pickles, milk and bread. Daniel's own hunger became more acute as he tried to turn his thoughts elsewhere. Stuffing their faces to their heart's content, they totally ignored the lady and the boy. To wash down his meal, the farmer pulled out a pitcher of wine and began drinking noisily. The overpowering smells of greasy meat and cheap wine mingled in the close air of the carriage, making Daniel's head spin queasily.

The farmer was greatly enjoying himself. "Uuh, excuse me, Your Excellency," he wheezed. "Forgot my manners for a minute. Puh-leeze, join me in a toast to our illustrious land."

"I was wondering when you were going to offer, young man," the Count snapped. "Still," he relented, "better late than never, I suppose." He held out a silver goblet. "Pour me a drink to the unification of Spain — and the driving out of all foreign elements: Jews, Moslems, and stray dogs, ha, ha, ha." The Count laughed uproariously at his own wit as he raised his cup to his lips.

At that moment, the lady lifted her veil. Her face was strikingly beautiful, despite the fact that she was middle-aged or even older. Her strong features might have been chiselled out of stone by a master sculptor. "Here, boy, take an apple," she said softly. Daniel held out his hand.

The count and the farmer watched with growing interest. After the apple came another. This was followed by some cake and something hot to drink. "Madame is too good to you, boy," sneered the Count. "Better enjoy it while you can, because you'll be coming with me soon — and I assure you, you won't be so pampered in *my* company."

The lady spoke. In a soft but commanding voice that held the accents of higher education, she said, "Your Excellency, do not trouble yourself. I am willing to take charge of the boy when we get to Madrid."

"Willing, Madame?" The Count looked taken aback. "Why are you willing? The boy is a scoundrel. No, Madame. With all due respect, I don't know what your plan is, but believe me, you are far better off leaving the likes of him alone..." He stopped speaking suddenly, eyes narrowing in suspicion. "Or is there perhaps another reason for your — how shall I say? — unusually strong interest?"

"No, of course not," she replied sternly. "I have no ulterior motive. He seems a good, polite boy. I am old and lonely. He will provide amusing company for a while. That is all."

The Count smiled contemptuously. "I do not grant your request. It does not appear to me as if you are in need of amusing company. Quite the contrary, you seem to be perfectly self-sufficient. Are you not?"

A little intoxicated, more than a little bored, the Count

continued to engage the woman in talk. There was a jeering note beneath the surface politeness of his remarks. The woman was careful to answer with dignity, but Daniel grew more and more nervous as the sparring continued. He kept his mouth firmly shut, and prayed silently for help — something, anything, to distract the Count.

The help came from an unexpected source. There was a sudden loud commotion outside. The Count turned to the window and peered out. A number of horsemen, soldiers of the king's army, rode alongside their carriage. Their leader bowed his head courteously, but spoke with authority.

"Count Rodriguez, we are here to escort you for the rest of the journey to ensure your safe arrival. The war in Granada grows fiercer every day. Your expertise is urgently required on the front."

Immediately, the atmosphere changed. The Count's chest swelled with self-importance. "I am needed at the front," he boomed at his fellow passengers. "I am the man of the hour!"

The rest of the journey passed quickly. Consumed with pride, the Count forgot about Daniel's existence, even though he sat directly opposite him. They reached Madrid, and the Count was about to leave with the soldiers when the disappointed farmer reminded him, "What about the boy, Your Excellency? Aren't you going to take him with you?"

Count Rodriguez paused by the carriage door. "No," he said regretfully. "A pity, I'd like nothing more than to see him grovel under my boots, but I can't be bothered with such things now. Time is of the essence."

He turned and, with an ironic bow, addressed himself to the lady. "He's all yours, Madame. Make sure he's a good Christian." He went off with the soldiers, bound for the battlefront, as a pair of strapping young men stepped up to speak in undertones with the mysterious lady.

The red-faced farmer shouted after the Count, "Wait, wait,

Your Excellency! I'll have him then..." Too late. His words trailed off into nothingness. Angrily, he turned to Daniel. "No matter. Come with me, boy. I could use an extra pair of hands."

Grabbing the boy by the arm, he started to pull fiercely. Daniel screamed. The two young men with the lady glanced in their direction, and came forward. One of them tapped the struggling farmer on the shoulder. "Unhand him, before I take you apart," he growled.

"Mind your own business — he's mine," the farmer gasped. "Let's go, brat!" Daniel stood his ground. The farmer pulled harder. In desperation, Daniel sank his teeth into the farmer's hand, almost taking out a chunk of calloused skin. The farmer yelped in fury and swung a wild fist in the boy's direction. Daniel ducked. The farmer went after him again, but before he got another chance the young man laid him low with a stunning right hook to the jaw.

"That should do it," he remarked to his companion. They turned away, leaving the farmer to lie on the ground until he regained enough strength to skulk away.

Daniel's rescuers brought him to the veiled lady. She inclined her head graciously. "Now that the entertainment's over, permit me to introduce myself. My name is Anne de Seville. These are two of my sons, Pancho and Fernando. We would be honored if you would accompany us to our home."

Daniel didn't hesitate. "Yes, ma'am."

Anne, a widow, lived with her two sons in a large house in one of Madrid's suburbs. Another son, he was told, was away on business. They were Marranos — outwardly practicing Christians, but privately the staunchest of Jews.

Even before arriving at their house, Daniel confided to Anne the true purpose of his coming to the city. She listened gravely. "As soon as I saw you, Daniel, my heart told me you were a Jew," she said, smiling sweetly. Then the smile disappeared and a look of determination replaced it. "Now we have to do something for your parents."

The widow knew of Uncle Sebastian and offered to make contact. To Daniel's frustration, she learned that he was out of town at the moment. His affairs were being conducted by a young man, Victor Condasta.

One afternoon he came to the de Seville home, a tall, dark gentleman with eyes that gave away nothing. He came to the point at once. "It will be far better for you, Daniel, to move in with me until your uncle returns."

Turning to Anne, Condasta added soberly, "We all know, don't we, Donna de Seville, that the Church is planning an investigation into your activities. Surely it would be unwise for the boy to remain here." Anne was reluctant to tell the boy what course to take. There was obviously sense in what the man said, but she knew nothing of his credentials. Could Condasta be trusted? Daniel would have to decide for himself.

What should he do?

Choice 1

Go with the man and hopefully accelerate the process of freeing his own parents. Turn to page 189.

Choice 2

Stay with Anne, at least until his uncle returns. Turn to page 194.

Bon Voyage!

On August 3, 1492, a fleet of ships comprising three vessels — the flagship, Santa Maria, the Pinta, and the Nina — weighed anchor in the Rio Tonto at Palos de la Frontera and sailed down the island of Saltes, to wait for a favorable wind. Commanding the flagship was forty-one-year-old Christopher Columbus, an Italian from the port city of Genoa. A sailor of great repute, he was also a renowned authority on chartmaking. Steeped in the knowledge of geography, astronomy and other sciences, Columbus was obsessed with the idea of sailing westward to the "Indies."

For years he sought sponsors for the giant undertaking. Rejected by his homeland and then by Portugal, Columbus finally found an enthusiastic benefactress in Queen Isabella. Buoyed by her recent victory in the ten-year-long war against the Moors of Granada, Isabella was ready to finance Columbus's voyage into the unknown.

Thus, with a total of eighty-seven seamen divided among the three ships, he began his quest.

Also on board were Pancho de Seville, serving as a midshipman on the Pinta, and Daniel Trigo, a galley-hand on the Nina.

It had not been an easy choice for Daniel. In the end, the chance of a lifetime for high adventure — the opportunity to explore strange new lands — had won the day. Sarah, his mother, used to say sometimes that if God had made her a man, she would have liked to have been a sailor, to see His world.

No questions were asked when Daniel was ushered on board. Since the crews had to be assembled hastily for what most people considered a dangerous mission, he had little difficulty in securing one of the four vacancies for young boys, whose job was to help prepare food and wash dishes. He lied about his age, though, saying he was fourteen.

"It is unfortunate that we are to be parted, but our ships will be in close contact," Pancho told him just before they separated. He clasped the boy's hand warmly. "Good luck."

Although already hard at work, Daniel could not resist the temptation to charge up on deck a short while after they set sail. The Spanish coastline was fast receding. A wave of exhilaration swept over him at the thrill of putting out to sea. Peering skyward, he marvelled at the large, sloping white sail, its width more than half the length of the ship. Two smaller sails helped provide wind power for the arduous journey ahead.

Alongside ranged the Pinta. Emblazoned in red on its mainsail was a huge cross. Leading the others was the Santa Maria. Among the other multi-colored banners, the flag of Isabella and Ferdinand fluttered proudly in the mild breeze.

"Come on, Trigo, this is no pleasure cruise. We have work to do!" The voice came gruff and booming. It was the cook, Alphonso, who towered over Daniel. At their first meeting, he'd eyed Daniel closely for some moments, as if summing him up. After a tense pause, he broke into a wide, toothy grin and gave

Daniel a firm handshake which almost cracked the boy's little knuckles. "Pleased to meet you. I'm sure we'll make a great team."

Daniel had taken an immediate liking to him, although, at times, he ranted and raved. The boy concluded that Alphonso's bark was far worse than his bite.

The seamen — mostly Basques and Andalusians — were a motley lot. They cared little for Columbus's noble quest. These sailors were lured by the promise of discovering gold and returning to their homes laden with riches and glory.

Daniel had decided to use his real name. Of course, he would not tell anyone he was Jewish, but then again, no-one seemed overly interested. It did happen, however, that much of the noisy chatter at meal-times revolved around the recent expulsion of the Jews.

He listened quietly as the uncouth sailors poured abuse on Jews and praised the turn of events.

"A great accomplishment it was," and "Good riddance to bad rubbish," were some of the comments that were freely bandied about. "I wish Pancho was on the Nina," Daniel fretted. "Then I'd have someone to really talk to." He began thinking more and more of his parents. Images of them sitting together at the Shabbos table appeared, and tore at his heart.

Still, there was scant time for self-pity. He was kept busy — too busy for thought — peeling vegetables, washing dishes, scrubbing floors, and, being the smallest, ordered about by the crew — until Alphonso put a stop to that.

"This lad works for me and nobody else. Is that clear to everybody?" he thundered. It became abundantly clear that the other sailors were to leave Daniel alone.

Daniel was curious about their journey. The sea looked the same on every side, stretching endlessly to the horizon. How would Columbus calculate in which direction to proceed? He brought his questions to Alphonso.

"Don't worry, lad," the cook boomed reassuringly. "There is no greater navigator in the whole world than the Admiral. Just by observing a cloud or star, he knows the direction to follow.

"Besides, there are all those maps and charts he works on day and night. He knows what he's doing!"

Daniel thought about Christopher Columbus. "There must be something special about him, seeing the way people talk of his deeds," he confided to Alphonso.

A steady north wind brought the fleet to the Canary Islands after a week at sea. Even after so short a time at sea, the view of the golden, mountainous shoreline at dawn was a feast for sore eyes, used to seeing only the never-ending choppy, blue waters of the sea.

Owing to the lack of a breeze, the ships were becalmed for two days between two smallish islands. Finally, the fleet entered the tiny port of Ferro.

During the stopover, the Pinta underwent minor repairs. This enabled Daniel and Pancho to meet. Excitedly they traded tales of their first week at sea.

In the meantime, many of the sailors got cold feet. The Islands were the last known habitable lands. Fear of the unknown spread like wildfire. "So what if there is gold for the taking? Of what use is it, if we won't live to enjoy it?" Such mutterings were fast becoming the only conversation heard on deck.

It took a certain Captain Martin Alonzo Pinzon to allay their fears. Captain Pinzon was a former pirate who was also a skilled navigator. He had personally recruited most of the sailors; now he went about reassuring them that they would return safely, and amazingly rich to boot. "You want to be poor for the rest of your lives? Fine, stay here and rot," he told them. Thanks to Pinzon, the sailors' fear was finally overcome by greed. Columbus prepared to sail again.

But before he did, a minor change took place in the crew.

One of the galley boys on the Santa Maria had fallen ill, and had to be left behind. Kind-hearted Alphonso was aware of Daniel's fascination with Columbus. Fond as he was of the boy, he recommended that he replace the sick galley-hand on the Santa Maria.

Daniel was hesitant, but he had to agree. Here was a man, he was sure, who would do something great, something that would go down in history. To serve on his ship would be something special.

Turn to page 180.

The Convert

ow can I go on a voyage now?" Daniel demanded. "For all I know, my parents are languishing in some prison."

Pancho sighed. "That's possible, Daniel. It's also possible that they left Spain during the Expulsion. Or perhaps, they are..."

"No, no, don't say it, Pancho! My parents are alive! They have to be!"

Pancho knew there was no use trying to persuade Daniel to join him. He shrugged. "Okay, do what you must."

"My uncle," Daniel thought aloud. "If I could locate him —"

"Who is your uncle?"

Daniel told him. Pancho nodded; he clearly knew the man.

"Your Uncle Sebastian disappeared at the time of the Expulsion. He knew all about your plight. In fact, it was through his good offices that I was able to locate you. I think the pressure of being a Marrano took its toll. He jumped at the opportunity to leave Spain and once again become, openly, a Jew."

Daniel was crestfallen. He had pinned a great deal of hope on his uncle. Without his help, how could he find out what had happened to his parents?

As if he'd read Daniel's thoughts, Pancho said slowly, "There is one man with the power to help you — Don Abraham Seneor."

Daniel looked at him in astonishment. "You mean the great Rabbi Seneor? But — how can that be? Surely he and the other sages, like Rabbi Abravanel, led the Jews out of Spain?"

"You're right. The others did leave. However, Don Seneor is still here. You have to remember that he is an old, old man. It's extremely difficult for him to get around."

Pancho sounded troubled, but Daniel did not want to pry into the reason. "So be it," he said decidedly. "I shall make contact with the great man. If anybody can help me, it is Rabbi Seneor."

Pancho started to speak, and then stopped. He hesitated, cleared his throat, and said, "Daniel, it is only right that you know."

"Know what?"

"Don Seneor has openly converted to Christianity."

Daniel dared not answer, for fear of what he might say. The rabbi had always been a court favorite, wielding great power and influence, especially with Queen Isabella. But he was first and foremost a Jew — a renowned *talmid chacham* and leader of his people.

"I don't believe it!" were the only words he could muster.

"I'm afraid it's true," Pancho said gravely. He leaned closer to the boy. "Listen to me, Daniel. Your one and only concern is finding out about your parents. He is your best bet. Go to him."

Daniel spent a troubled night, but in the morning he'd made his decision. He would put his personal feelings aside and take his friend's advice. Pancho supplied him with a set of new clothing and an ample amount of money. Clasping hands, they wished each other luck — Pancho, for a safe and successful voyage, and Daniel in tracking down his beloved parents. Daniel turned resolutely and set off for the home of Don Seneor.

The name of his Uncle Sebastian was the key that got him an interview with the man he sought.

"Come in, little chap, come in," Don Seneor called out. Daniel ventured timidly into the study, not knowing what to expect. The walls were lined with books, all of them of a religious or historical nature. Pride of place went to a beautifully bound set of Talmud with rich crimson leather covers, flanked by numerous writings of the sages.

He stood up to welcome Daniel. Short and stocky, he wore a plain black suit over a white, frilly shirt. He had a trim white beard, a deeply wrinkled face and a look of sadness in his eye that belied his jovial manner. Around his neck hung a tiny cross. So it was true, thought Daniel. He had switched faiths.

"You say your name is Daniel Trigo, nephew of my dear friend, Sebastian Santos."

Daniel nodded. He didn't trust himself to speak.

"What can I do for you?" Don Seneor said, smiling.

Daniel was still having a hard time finding his tongue, so Don Seneor added helpfully, "I take it you are a Marrano?"

"No. No...uuh...uuh...rabbi...I mean, Don Seneor."

The old man frowned. "You may call me rabbi," he said softly. "Now then, if you are not a Marrano, who are you?"

"I am a Jew, Rabbi."

"A Jew — but that's impossible! All the Jews have been expelled. None remain..."

Daniel watched the old man struggling to speak. His face reddened, and he barely managed a pitiful choke. The eyes, already watery, filled with tears. "Excuse me, Daniel, I am an old man. At my age, we cry a lot."

Daniel waited. If he was a Christian, would he be unwilling to tell him anything about his family? One question revolved over and over in his head: How was it possible for such a great *tzaddik* to have done what he did?

The answer revealed itself in the tears. They spoke of the profound conflict in the old man's soul.

Daniel finally let the words flow. "Rabbi, my parents were arrested about a year ago in Allerema. The Church wanted me also, but I got away."

All at once his feelings overflowed, and he let his tears flow — a release he had not allowed himself since his whole ordeal had begun. Together, they cried. Don Seneor collected himself first. He placed a hand on Daniel's shoulders. Warmth and kindness, like those of a compassionate grandfather, radiated from the old man.

"Take your time, my boy," he said gently. "It is possible I can help you." Daniel, between the tears, related his story in detail, adding his belief that his Uncle Sebastian had had the means to bring about their freedom.

Midway through his story, Don Seneor let out a sudden shout. It turned out to be a cheer of jubilation!

"Oh, how old and feeble I am becoming. My memory must be failing me. How could I have forgotten?" His grip on the boy's shoulder tightened so that Daniel winced. "My dear boy, your parents are safe and well — here in Madrid!"

Daniel was speechless. He felt weak, numb, strong, exuberant, joyous and bewildered, all at the same time.

"Let me explain," Don Senior said quickly. "Ooh, I still can't believe how I could have forgotten! Daniel, shortly before the Expulsion your uncle, Sebastian, told me he had gotten word that his brother and wife were prisoners in Allerema. At first he hoped to have them freed by his own resources. But the situation worsened. Your parents were condemned to death by the Church. Sebastian came to me. I was his last recourse.

"At the time, I was unwell and could do nothing. But by a strange quirk of fate, we were later informed the Trigos were being kept alive by a certain priest. His name eludes me. Wait a minute, it's on the tip of my tongue. Yes, that's it! I remember now — Diego. Fray Antonio Diego." He didn't notice Daniel's start at the sound of that name.

"Word filtered through that just days, if not hours, before the executions were to have been held, your mother was taken gravely ill. In reality, she was expecting a baby."

"What!" exclaimed Daniel. "I don't believe it! I am an only child, Rabbi. My father used to tell me that God willed it so..." He looked thunderstruck.

Don Seneor smiled. "It seems God had other ideas. Allow me to continue. Diego stayed the executions. Apparently, he wanted to wait until your mother gave birth before he had your parents killed. He would bring up the baby as a loyal Christian. That would have been his ultimate victory.

"However, the Expulsion and I intervened. I recovered from my illness and managed to use my influence to free them. The Expulsion decree also hastened their release and departure for Madrid, much to the chagrin of the priest.

"They were to leave Spain with the rest of the Jews, but it became too difficult for your mother to travel." He smiled again. "I have a sneaking suspicion that, in any case, they wouldn't have gone anywhere until they'd found you." Don Senior paused. "Your mother and father are being looked after at the home of a friend."

"Oh, Rabbi, take me to them. Please!" Daniel hardly dared let himself feel the joy that flooded him from top to bottom.

"Yes. Let us go — now."

Outside, Daniel was surprised to see that it was already twilight. The air was cool. He thought of God, who directed all things, and of how his life had turned full circle. A feeling of contentment such as he'd never experienced welled up inside him.

Daniel waited outside nervously, while the old rabbi entered the house. David Trigo welcomed him. He was paler and thinner than he'd once been, and there was a discouraged look in his eye.

"There is someone, Don Trigo, who wishes to see you."

"To see me?" David summoned a smile. "Please, whoever it is, tell him to come in."

The door opened. For an electric instant father and son gazed upon each other. Then Daniel charged forward, straight into his father's arms. David thought of Jacob's reunion with his long-lost son, Joseph, and how he had recited the *Shema* in gratitude. Daniel cried as he kissed his father over and over again.

At the commotion, Sarah, obviously in an advanced stage of pregnancy, came slowly into the room. Her eyes widened at the sight of her husband hugging a little boy. She gasped — it was her Daniel. She almost flew to join them. With a cry, Daniel threw his arms around his mother. Their laughter and tears lasted a long time. No one noticed when Don Seneor slipped from the room, a small, happy smile on his face.

A short time later a beautiful baby girl was born to the Trigos. They named her Bracha, for she had made her presence known when all had seemed lost and had brought a blessing to their home.

The Trigos soon left Spain and made the journey to Italy, where David became a notable dignitary of the Jewish community in Genoa. Their descendants were drawn to the learning houses of Eastern Europe and right before catastrophe struck in the form of the Holocaust, they migrated to America. Finally, the dynasty settled in *Eretz Yisrael*.

But long before all these later generations came into being, Daniel Trigo asked his father a very important question. How was it that such a great *tzaddik* as Rabbi Seneor had converted to Christianity?

"He probably didn't tell you, my son, because he did not want to make excuses. It has been said that the king and queen threatened to wipe whole Jewish communities from the face of Spain if he remained a Jew.

"Based on that, he made a decision," David Trigo ended. "It is not for us to judge."

The End

The New World

Life on the Nina had been rough, but it was mere child's play compared to what Daniel endured on the flagship. The cook and his first assistant regarded him as their personal slave. But all his sufferings flew out of Daniel's mind when, at long last, he received the order he'd been longing for. "The admiral wants to see you in his quarters."

It was Columbus's policy to acquaint himself with every member of the crew, and it had already been three days since leaving the Canary Islands.

"Ugh! I look so shabby and dirty — and my hair is so long and snarled! What will he think?" Daniel wanted to make a good impression. Here was a man who swayed the decisions of kings.

"Maybe...Just maybe..." Somewhere in the back of his mind a ray of light flickered continuously and refused to die. His parents were alive, and Columbus just might be the one to help find them.

When Daniel entered the cramped cabin cluttered with every imaginable navigational instrument, the admiral rose to his full height and stuck out a hand in greeting. "Aah, Daniel Trigo. I've heard only good things about you, my boy. My name is Christopher Columbus."

Daniel awkwardly held out his hand. He looked up at the tall man hovering over him. Columbus had rich brown eyes and white hair which made him look far older than he was. The distinguished face was pensive and unsmiling, as if the admiral was deep in thought even as he spoke.

Daniel had carefully rehearsed his lines. "It is a great pleasure to serve on your ship, sir."

"Thank you. I'm happy to have you on board. Tell me son, are you being treated properly by the crew? They can be rough on the young ones, I know."

Since he hadn't been harmed physically, what was the point of complaining? Daniel's father had drummed into his head the pitfalls of bearing tales against others. "No, sir. I have no complaints."

"Very good, then." Columbus smiled for the first time. "Well, join me in a drink to a successful mission." Pouring a tot of rum for the both of them, he proposed a toast. Thus ended Daniel's first meeting with the admiral.

It was about then that the rumblings began.

The crew was restless. Though the air was mild and the seas stayed calm, the atmosphere on board was filled with tension. The superstitious sailors gaped in horror one night as a meteor crossed the sky in a flaming ball of fire. " 'Tis an evil omen!" they cried. From then on, they took anything out of the ordinary to mean pending disaster.

A steady trade wind from the east kept the sails billowing ahead towards the unknown. "The wind will never change course and take us back home," they lamented. "We are doomed."

Most frightening of all were the birds. Day and night they

...a meteor crossed the sky in a flaming ball of fire.
" 'Tis an evil omen!" they cried.

flew overhead as if waiting patiently for death to come to the ships.

Even a cause for joyous celebration — the sighting of land — turned to dismay when Captain Pinzon of the Pinta, desiring the promised reward money for being the first to discover land, mistakenly took a cloud formation for a shoreline.

Columbus watched the signs of discontent in silence. One starlit night, as was his habit, he walked on deck alone. A young boy, exhausted and ill, sat hunched in a corner leaning against one of the masts.

"Aah, if it isn't young Daniel," said Columbus. He gave the boy a wry smile. "It seems to me that you look on the outside the way I feel on the inside."

Daniel, startled by the admiral's sudden appearance, struggled weakly to his feet. "I'll be all right, sir. I'm just a little under the weather, that's all."

Columbus leaned against the railing and began to talk in a soft voice. Daniel listened, raptly. He could hardly believe his good fortune — that the great admiral had singled *him* out for his confidences. In the glow of starlight shimmering off the sea, a bond was woven between the explorer and young Jew.

"The poor sailors, how blind they are," said Columbus. "So often, I've told them that birds — petrels, terns, pelicans — flying overhead is a sign that land is near. There are also the field birds on their annual southward migration. But they don't want to listen."

His voice quickened. "Yesterday, Daniel, I saw a branch with flowers and a stick floating in the water. We are close — so close. In fact, I am reminded of the story of Noah and the ark, when the dove brought back a fig-leaf to let his master know that the flood was over."

Listening to Columbus made Daniel forget his exhaustion. The mention of Noah stirred the boy's soul. He was even more moved by Columbus's following remark.

"Sometimes I see you with a small, black book. From afar, it looks like a prayer-book of sorts." Columbus probed him with keen eyes. "You're Jewish, aren't you?"

Daniel hesitated. But before he could say anything, Columbus held up a hand. "Hush, hush, don't tell me. It is better to hold onto one's secrets. Let me just say that I, too, strive to be of a religious bent. Seeing the magnificence of God's universe, how can one be otherwise?"

Daniel listened to the admiral enthralled, like a youngster seated on his father's lap, warmed by wondrous tales. But all too soon, the spell was shattered when a tipsy sailor stumbled by, cursing and muttering. Columbus looked after him. "I fear I may have to do something drastic to avoid a mutiny," he said in a low voice.

Daniel said nothing, but he was filled with unease.

The next morning, Columbus changed course. The sailors thought he'd done this to pacify them, when in actuality, he had observed great armies of birds flying north to southwest. Portuguese discoverers had spoken of sighting similar bird patterns before striking land.

Four days later, in heavy seas, he changed course once again — this time due west. The admiral, standing majestically on the sterncastle that night, made out a bobbing light which came into view and then disappeared on the horizon. Five hours later, land was spotted by a sailor on the Pinta.

The area, extending between the Gulf of Mexico and the Caribbean Sea, became known as the Antilles.

Maneuvering between craggy reefs, the three ships found an opening. Waiting and watching with disbelieving eyes on the rocky beach were men, women and children, all with reddish brown skins, and all stark naked.

Out of the sea came the strangers. To the natives they must have seemed like something out of a dream. They watched as Columbus stepped off the boat onto land and, together with his

Out of the sea came the strangers.

men, kissed the ground and praised God for bringing them there in safety. Bearing the royal standard, they staked a claim on the land on behalf of the King and Queen of Spain.

The admiral was to learn that the islanders called their home Guanahoni. He renamed it San Salvador. Then he and his crew set sail again throughout the area known today as the Bahamas. They sailed for ninety-six days, and in each new territory, Columbus made the same claim. From this time on, the land would belong to Spain.

Daniel, like the others, was caught up in the excitement. After a while, however, the sailors became disenchanted with the natives' offerings of glass beads, small ornaments and sparkling amulets. Where was the gold?

Captain Pinzon, crazed for wealth, heard of a beach where gold was gathered in abundance at night by candlelight. Flaunting the admiral's authority, he ordered the Pinta's crew to hoist sail and follow the trail of the gold. As a member of the crew, Pancho had no choice but to go along.

Another mishap occurred soon afterwards. While Columbus was taking a rare nap, the Santa Maria went aground on a reef and had to be abandoned. A garrison of men stayed behind and built a fort in the new territory.

Columbus and Daniel sailed back to Spain on the Nina.

The ship returned to Spain in triumph. In Barcelona, Ferdinand and Isabella gave the courageous explorers a hero's welcome. The Pinta returned later, on its own. Thinking that his ship had preceded Columbus, Captain Pinzon was so upset to hear that the Nina had beaten him to Spain that he suffered a heart attack and died.

The Nina sailors were famous. Even Daniel became somewhat of a celebrity. Snatching a moment together amid the celebration, Columbus confided in his young friend.

"I'll let you in on a secret. I kept two logs of distances we sailed — one for the crew, and one for myself. In the first I wrote figures that were less than we actually sailed."

Daniel was bewildered. "But — why?"

Columbus smiled. "The further from home they believed they had traveled, the unhappier the sailors would become. I, alone, knew how far we actually went." The admiral and the boy laughed together. Then Daniel drew a deep breath and met Columbus's eyes.

"I, too, have a secret," he confessed. "The time has come to tell you." He told the story of his heritage, his parents, and his burning desire to find them.

Columbus was a man of action. Without delay he saw to it that the length and breadth of Spain was combed to discover any trace of the Trigos' whereabouts. The trail came to an abrupt end with Fray Antonio Diego.

Yielding to the forces arrayed against him, the priest reluctantly revealed that David and Sarah Trigo had gone to Italy. In the wave of the Jewish exodus, he had been unable to have them executed. He'd had his chance before the Expulsion, but had waited too long.

With help from virtually the entire Spanish nobility, Daniel was able to leave Spain for a second time. He bid the country a bittersweet farewell. He had made many new friends, not least of them Christopher Columbus — but Spain was no longer a place for Jews. The Golden Age was over.

In Italy, the Jews had settled in two basic areas. After a brief but hectic search, Daniel found his parents, David and Sarah. The couple — who had resigned themselves with deep sorrow to the loss of their beloved only son — praised their Creator for reuniting them once more. "God is good and just," David Trigo exulted. And his wife could not agree more.

Astonished, they listened to Daniel's account of his amazing adventures with Christopher Columbus. The explorer had proved himself a staunch friend to the boy. He was also, Daniel told his parents, a deeply religious Christian.

"Columbus?" his father echoed thoughtfully. "You know, there was a Marrano family by that name."

"No, I didn't know," Daniel said, his heart beating a little faster. Maybe...Just maybe...Who knew?

The End

Betrayed

ictor noticed Daniel's uncertainty. He leaned closer to the boy, speaking persuasively.

"Donna de Seville has told me all about you. You must trust me, Daniel. It is true I am a loyal Catholic. But amongst our flock are many who hold the Jews in the highest esteem.

"Just think about it. Your uncle would never have hired me to work for him if I was sympathetic to the Inquisition. With me, rest assured you will be safe... But by staying here with Donna de Seville, who is a known Marrano, you put yourself in grave danger."

Daniel searched Donna de Seville's face for a sign, or a gesture, telling him what to do.

But she remained expressionless. This Victor was right, she was thinking. She could not guarantee Daniel's safety, and he could. That was the important thing.

And yet, she was not at all sure the man could be trusted...

The boy turned again to Victor. He certainly seemed honest enough. Besides — most important of all — Donna de Seville had said that Victor spoke of friends in high places who could help secure his parents' release.

"All right," said Daniel. "I shall come with you, sir."

The man beamed as if he'd won a major victory. "Please call me Victor," he urged, shaking the boy's hand vigorously.

For the next week, Daniel was showered with hospitality. He was given a room in what appeared to be a combination of living and office quarters. During the day and much of the night, he listened to the sounds of the busy, bustling city beneath his window. The only thing that disturbed him was that Victor insisted he stay out of sight.

Sebastian's assistant was usually close by to ease Daniel's loneliness. As time went by, he sat more and more with the boy, discussing, mostly, religious matters. He didn't seem to mind, or to remember, that Daniel was only eleven.

"It doesn't really make any difference what a person believes, so long as he believes in something," Victor said with his genial smile.

"Well, I think there is a lot of truth in what you're saying. I remember my father telling me that one of our great Jewish sages, Maimonides, was of the opinion that God made the religions for man to believe in something."

"Aah, I'm glad we're in agreement!"

Daniel became uncomfortable when Victor one day brought a copy of the New Testament and began quoting from its pages.

"Understand, Daniel, I am not trying to prove that the Christian faith is the ultimate truth. I only want to open your mind to its possibilities..." Victor assured him.

"Victor, I don't think I want to hear any of that," Daniel protested. "My Torah is enough for me."

Victor leaned over emphatically. "But these verses I want you to read are clear and uncomplicated. They can only be of benefit in helping you find the truth. It's because I am so fond of you that I care about your eternal life."

Daniel wanted to tell him that as far as he was concerned he already knew where the truth lay and was not interested in looking elsewhere. He tried to change the subject. "Have you found out anything about my parents yet?"

Victor's answer was the same as ever. "Don't worry yourself. I have my people working on it twenty-four hours a day. I am hopeful that in next to no time they will be free — possibly even before your uncle returns from his business trip."

On the seventeenth day in the apartment, Daniel had just finished lunch when Victor entered his room. Behind him was an even taller man whose bald head, like a polished dome, loomed large and forbidding.

Daniel's heart sank. He had only seen the man once, and then from a distance, on the day his parents were taken prisoner. Unmistakably, the head belonged to Fray Antonio Diego.

Daniel sat bolt upright. "I have been betrayed!" was all he could manage to scream.

Victor ignored his outburst. Turning to the priest, he said in his suave voice, "Father, believe me, I tried. With love in my heart, I implored the boy to take heed, but the truth was locked out of his soul. At last, I felt it my duty to inform the Church."

Victor's deception was out in the open now. He had wiled his way into the confidence of the extremely cautious Sebastian. His task was to discover whether Sebastian — as some suspected — was indeed living the life of a secret Jew.

Sebastian was smart. He gave nothing away, not even to his trusted right-hand man. Then the prize had fallen into Victor's lap: Sebastian's young nephew, Daniel Trigo. Now the wrath of the Church could be unleashed on David Trigo's brother as well.

Fray Diego, too, was delighted. "I've waited long to catch

up with you, young Trigo. My revenge on all Jews will soon be complete. Mark my words!"

Without further ado, Daniel was removed from his shelter and returned to Allerema — as a prisoner. He was to be reunited with his parents, but not in the way he'd dreamed of for so long.

Fray Diego's men dumped him into a small, stuffy dungeon where some thirty other Jews awaited execution.

It took a few minutes in the semi-darkness for David and Sarah Trigo to grasp what was happening. Impossible to move with any degree of freedom, they at first showed little interest in yet another newcomer joining their ranks.

And then in a low voice, a boy called out, "Mamma, Poppa. Are you here? It's me, Daniel."

A path opened up out of nowhere. Daniel was crushed in a tight and tearful embrace. He and his mother and father were together again.

It didn't take Daniel long to learn that they were all soon to be executed. He, a child, had earned the dubious honor of being accorded the status of a "criminal" adult.

But Fray Diego was not through with him yet. Daniel was of an age where he was considered a good prospect for conversion. The priest offered him a life of bliss within the Church. "Otherwise," he said harshly, his dark eyes glittering in the semi-darkness, "you will perish with all the other fools, including your mother and father."

Daniel answered by pressing closer to his beloved mother. With every ounce of courage he had he answered, "I may be only eleven, but when I get to the Next World that won't make any difference. My soul will be close to God. I am staying."

In the early hours of the morning, just two days before the mass hanging was to take place, a fire broke out in the prison.

Anne de Seville (who herself had come under close scrutiny since she had taken Daniel under her wing) had activated a vast network of underground agents to help the condemned prisoners. She recruited the help of Sebastian, too, who called Victor to him and threatened him in no uncertain manner. The young man, a coward at heart, conveniently disappeared from the scene the instant he felt his own life was in danger.

A great deal of money and effort went into arranging the fire. The enterprise was perhaps the first time that an action was taken against the Church. It provided hope for future resistance against persecution and injustice.

Once the fire took hold, its flames spread with lightning speed. The wooden prison structure was rapidly devoured. Chaos broke out as guards and inmates alike fled in all directions. The Trigos, determined to stay together, contended with flying debris and blazing heat. Daniel coughed and choked in the thick smoke, tears streaming down his cheeks. Desperately he held onto his father's shirt as fear-crazed figures pushed past him. Just when he was on the verge of being driven apart from his parents, a group of people led by his uncle Sebastian appeared miraculously out of the dense smoke and hauled them to safety. Apart from minor burns and cuts, the family emerged unscathed.

For the next few months, many Jews lived in hiding. Among them were David, Sarah and Daniel Trigo. Then came the Expulsion Edict, proclaiming that all Jews must leave Spain's borders. For some, it proved a blessing in disguise. Now the Jews could at last escape the Church's clutches.

For the likes of Fray Diego and his kind, it robbed them of a favorite pursuit: hounding and torturing Jews. Now their victims were to go far away from their sticky net.

Daniel and his parents, together with other Jews travelled to Amsterdam. There, far from the Spain they loved, but which had brought them such sorrow, they hoped to begin a brand new life.

The End.

Destiny

Daniel was sorely tempted. Since the arrest of his parents, he had kept on the move. He was so tired... Surely, by entering his uncle's home, he was taking a step in the right direction. So what if Sebastian was not around. He would be safe in the hands of someone who worked for him. Wouldn't he?

Yet something about Victor Condasta did not appear 100 percent right. Daniel could not put his finger on it. Most probably, it was nothing and the young man was a genuine, loyal ally of Sebastian's.

Daniel's gaze rested on Anne de Seville, who had taken him under her protection. He made up his mind. Sometimes it was better to stay put. Moving on was no guarantee of success. He trusted Donna de Seville. She reminded him of his own grandmother, his father's mother, who was taken from the family so suddenly during a plague when he was only seven. His grandma, when she died, had been about the same age as Donna de Seville was now. He turned to face Victor Condasta.

"Thank you very much Don Condasta, but I will stay here until my uncle's return."

"But, but —" Victor spluttered. "Think again! How can I get it into your head that the Church has for a long time suspected Donna de Seville of being a secret Jew? They will find you here and arrest you!"

Now that Daniel had come to a decision, Anne was there to help defend it. "Sir, I am sorry to say this but I cannot accept this slur against my name. All *conversos* are closely watched. But I have nothing to hide. I am a devout Christian who a long, long time ago unfortunately happened to be a Jew. One beautiful day, thanks to pious, upstanding ministers of the Church, I saw the light and realized I had to rid myself of a false religion. I shall always be grateful." She drew herself up and added, "I am in high standing with Torquemada himself. If this boy wishes to stay with me, he may do so."

"Then answer one question," snapped Victor. "If you are such a loyal Christian and you also know that he is wanted by the Church, what right have you to hide him?"

Sternly, she shot back, "Sir, I ask the same question of you. If you are a Catholic, why do *you* want to protect him?"

"Huh, that's easy. I am in the employ of Sebastian Santos. It is obvious that he is not a true convert...But be that as it may, I will not be the one to betray him and send him to his death." He smirked. "I know I am taking a chance, but I also know on what side my bread is buttered."

"It is no business of yours to pry into my private life," Anne retorted. "All I'm doing is permitting the boy to stay here until his uncle returns. Then it will be up to Don Santos take the next step."

Seeing that he was making no headway in persuading Daniel, Victor turned abruptly on his heel and left.

Daniel remained under the protective wing of Anne de Seville. In the days to come great changes took place affecting every Jew in Spain. The Expulsion was decreed and — not for the first time in their history — Jews were exiled from their homes, to scatter to the four corners of the earth.

Among them was one young boy by the name of Daniel Trigo.

What became of Daniel?

We move ahead exactly five hundred years later to the year 1992. An eleven-year-old boy, of Brooklyn, New York in the United States of America, happened to pick up a copy of his daily newspaper. He read a special invitation issued by the Spanish Royal Family and addressed to world Jewry:

In commemoration of the infamous expulsion of the Jews from Spain five hundred years ago, the people of this fair land invite members of that faith to return in peace.

"Phew, that's weird. I'd really like to know what went on over there," the boy remarked. That evening, he showed the article to his father.

"It seems to me, son, that the Spaniards regret what occurred during that period," his father said. "By making this gesture, they probably intend to somehow undo all the persecution.

"I don't know too much about what happened," he continued, "but if you're so interested, I can try to get hold of some reading material on the subject. A great deal has been recorded, both historical fact and fiction."

The boy listened intently as his father described the calamities of that distant age. What he heard only served to whet his appetite for further information. From that day on he devoured any book he could get on the subject.

Late one night, while lying in bed, the boy was reading

parts of an old, frayed textbook relating to Spain in the fifteenth and sixteenth centuries. The words bounced in and out of his tired vision. The book, becoming heavier and heavier, was about to drop from his hands.

It was then that he made the discovery. Buried somewhere on the tattered pages was the following paragraph:

David and Sarah Trigo: One of the most influential families from the province of Andalusia in pre-united Spain. Braving harsh conditions and weathering threatening decrees issued by the Church, they remained full-fledged Jews. Born to them was one son, Daniel. Some reports mentioned a daughter, but this was not verified. No trace of her name has been found.

The boy was suddenly very, very wide awake. His head spun dizzily and his insides shivered — and all for good reason. For his own name was Daniel Trigo, son of David Trigo.

Fingers trembling in anticipation, he turned the page. A second paragraph read:

The family's luck eventually ran out and they were arrested not long before the Expulsion. The fate of the parents remains unknown, but Daniel apparently left with thousands of Jews and Marranos to other lands. It was said that he became one of the great spiritual leaders of his generation.

That was all.

The next evening, Daniel approached his father. "Dad, do we have a family tree going back to our roots?"

"Yes, Daniel, we do. About eight or nine years ago, we had one made. You were just a toddler then, so it wouldn't have concerned you at the time. I'd just about forgotten about it."

"Dad, how far back were you able to trace?" Daniel persisted eagerly.

"Let's see. I seem to remember seven generations, going back to Eastern Europe. Poland, actually, was the furthest from the present. Also, you are already the third generation in the States. Why the sudden interest? Any particular reason?"

Daniel produced the book.

"Here, read these two paragraphs!"

Intrigued, his father took the book from his hand.

"Be careful, Dad, the pages are loose. Hold it carefully, please!"

"Okay, okay, son," came the reply. "Don't get excited." He read the contents...once, twice, three times.

"Wow! Interesting, very interesting. What an amazing co-incidence!"

"Coincidence! Dad, that's no coincidence. You yourself have always taught me there's no such thing as coincidence."

"Right, Daniel, there isn't. But that doesn't necessarily mean because those two names correspond to our names there is a connection. In the Jewish world, Daniel and David are pretty common...and we are not the only Trigos around."

"Dad, they were our direct ancestors." Daniel spoke with perfect conviction. "Our great, great, grandfathers — or whatever. I just know it!"

Two years passed. Further investigation by the family did indeed reveal that their line probably went back to fifteenth-century Spain, but they failed to find absolute proof. Daniel remained convinced that he was directly descended from the Trigos of the textbook — so much so, that he persuaded his parents to travel via Spain when they made their first family visit to Israel.

Four days were spent touring parts of the Iberian Penin-sula, including Allerema, Seville and Madrid. Aside from the extraordinary beauty of the country, Daniel found the people and places hauntingly fascinating. His disappointment at their short stay was pushed aside at the realization that their next stop was Israel, home of Abraham, Isaac and Jacob. Upon arrival, the Trigos made a beeline for Jerusalem, the holiest city of all.

The boy immediately felt spiritually elevated. It was as if the joy he'd felt in Spain found expression at the Western Wall and the other holy places. There and then, he decided he was going to live in Israel as soon as possible.

That very night, Daniel had a vivid dream he would never forget. Some of the areas he had recently been through in Spain formed the backdrop, but no modern inventions such as cars, electric lights or up-to-date dress were to be seen anywhere.

A mysterious, veiled lady weaved in and out of a confusing series of adventures. Constantly at her side was a young boy. The two of them persevered through thick and thin, before they finally escaped together to a far-off land.

The most uncanny thing of all was the way the boy in the dream resembled Daniel, the dreamer. They were as identical as twins.

The End